THE MATZO MITZVAH

The *MATZO MITZVAH*

Even More Tales My Great-Great-Grandfather Might Tell About Life in a Ghetto of Russia in the Time of the Czars

By
Herman I. Kantor
with Eric Larson

Illustrated by Jan Golden

Fithian Press • Santa Barbara, California • 1996

This is a work of fiction. Any resemblance to real events or to real persons, living or dead, is truly to be regretted.

Copyright © 1996 Herman I. Kantor
All Rights Reserved
Printed in the United States of America

Published by Fithian Press
A division of Daniel and Daniel, Publishers, Inc.
Post Office Box 1525
Santa Barbara, CA 93102

Design by Eric Larson

LIBRARY OF CONGRESS CATALOGING-IN-PUBLICATION DATA
Kantor, Herman I.
    The matzo mitzvah : even more tales my great-great-grandfather might tell about life ina ghetto of Russia in the time of the czars / Herman I. Kantor, with Eric Larson.
       p. cm.
    ISBN 1-56474-178-8 (alk. paper)
      1. Jews—Russia—Social life and customs—Fiction. 2. Jews—Russia—History—Fiction. I. Larson, Eric, 1956–   II. Title.
PS3561.A515M38 1996
813'.54—dc20   96-8331
                                                    CIP

*Dedicated to the memory of
my great-great-grandfather,
Rabbi Shmul,
who presented many of
the ideas for these stories
to me and my imagination.*

CONTENTS

The Cow Who Ate Meat	11
My Fellow Ghettoites	25
The Salesman's Donation	39
Frum	55
Sherlock Shmul	65
The Stranger	77
The Hat in the Horse Trough	87
The Rabbi's Shabbes Shoes	97
Not Guilty	107
The Matzo Mitzvah	121
The Rabbi and the Soldier	133

THE MATZO MITZVAH

*Even More Tales My Great-Great-Grandfather
Might Tell About Life in a Ghetto of Russia
in the Time of the Czars*

The Cow Who Ate Meat

Reb Chaim ben Itzik was a dairy farmer, and one of the leaders of the ghetto community in Orsha. Reb Chaim was a member of the ghetto's ad-hoc council, and often contributed his wise and thoughtful advice on the many thorny issues facing the shtetl. But who would advise Reb Chaim when it was suspected that the milk from his beautiful Jersey cows might not be kosher?

No one had ever doubted the purity of the milk sold by Reb Chaim. Its color was whiter than the clouds, whiter than new snow, whiter than the thoughts of a newborn babe. Moreover, it was so rich with cream that one tall glass of it would fill the emptiest belly. "Like butter!" his wife, Mirscha, would exclaim. Indeed, it was not only savored by the Jews of the ghetto, who knew without doubt that it was prepared in strict kosher tradition, but also on occasion by the village Russians, who cared nothing for koshreth but who loved a glass of rich, pure milk as much as anyone. Therefore the Russians didn't even take notice when the Jews of the Orsha ghetto suddenly became concerned that this wonderful milk might not be kosher after all.

It happened this way: One fine spring morning, the dew still sparkling on the grass, Reb Chaim was making the rounds of his pastures to see how his cows were faring. Just a week ago he had inoculated them with the new Pasteur vaccine, after some very heated discussion in the council as to whether this would be allowable, and he wanted to see if he noticed any reaction to the vaccine. It being spring, he was also on the lookout for any cows that might be coming into heat and ready to breed.

All the animals looked fine—robust, healthy and fattening diligently on the lush new grass. And, sure enough, one cow in particular, the one named Betzik, who was a favorite of his wife, Mirscha, was as nervous as a bride under the chuppa. It was her time, all right.

For breeding, Reb Chaim's cows relied on the services of the steers living in the adjacent lot, which were owned by a Russian man, Gorig Gorovitch, who raised them for beef. They were huge, virile animals, and more than once Reb Chaim had had to pay Gorig Gorovitch a stud fee in arrears after one of them had torn down the fence in order to pass a pleasant hour with one of his heifers. It was a mitzvah in disguise, though, because it was a lot of work to round up a bull and a cow, put them in a pen together, and hope that they took to each other, which they didn't always. It was actually a lot easier to just repair the hole in the fence.

The only problem was with one particular bull, one so ornery and full of mischief that Reb Chaim didn't trust it with his "ladies." That bull was named Vordor, and he had a long forelock and a white star on his forehead that made him look even meaner if that was possible, more unpredictable than he really was. Vordor was a terror to Gorig Gorovitch. He had broken down stalls in the barn, he had uprooted trees in the pasture, and he had even killed another bull once while vying for the attentions of one of Reb Chaim's cows. Gorig kept him as a stud, however, because the cows just couldn't resist him—they probably didn't dare—and because Vordor was now so old, tough, and ornery that he wouldn't have brought a decent price at market, anyway.

But that wasn't why Reb Chaim distrusted the bull Vordor. What concerned Reb Chaim and actually made him a little afraid of Vordor was a habit the bull had that neither Reb Chaim nor Gorig Gorovitch would have believed, had they not seen it themselves: the bull ate meat.

The first time they saw it, they thought the animal must be mad. They were leaning on their respective sides of the fence between their lots, discussing the weather and the state of their herds, when all of a sudden Vordor sprang into a frenzy.

"I don't care what those so-called scientists in Moscow say," Gorig Gorovitch was saying, "you can't get a bull to come on command, no matter how—now, what in the world…?"

The bull Vordor had jumped up from where he'd been lying in the sun, and was tearing around the pasture as though the very devil were in him, pawing at the ground, thrashing the air with his horns, and sending up a terrific cloud of dust. Gorig Gorovitch quickly jumped over onto Reb Chaim's side of the fence to avoid being bowled over as Vordor came charging by; and as the bull passed, both men saw that he was chasing a gopher.

"Go get 'im, boy!" Gorig Gorovitch called, taken by the excitement, as his bull careened around the corner of the lot in hot pursuit of the frantic gopher.

"Go get him," Reb Chaim chimed in.

The bull and the gopher ran straight across the

lot, zigged and zagged and spun around, and charged off in the opposite direction. They wheeled and darted, ran and dashed, and then the gopher made a mistake. It had spun around so many times it must have been dizzy, for it ran right at the enraged bull. Quick as a wink, Vordor caught the rodent with one neat swing of his head, impaled it on his right horn, and flipped it up into the air. To the amazement of both Reb Chaim and Gorig Gorovitch, Vordor caught the flailing gopher in his mouth and swallowed it whole!

Vordor stood panting in the middle of the pasture, and Reb Chaim and Gorig Gorovitch just stared at him.

"My God," said Gorig Gorovitch. "He ate it! I've never seen such a thing in my entire life!"

"This is not good, Gorig Gorovitch," said Reb Chaim. "It's unnatural. Bulls aren't supposed to eat gophers. They're supposed to eat grass and hay like a normal bull, not chase around like meshugge after gophers. I hope he doesn't get sick. You'd better keep an eye on him, Gorig Gorovitch."

They stood there for a while to see if Vordor would do it again, but when nothing happened after half an hour, they parted and went home. Gorig Gorovitch watched the animal closely after that, and never saw a repeat of this amazing performance. But he did continue to find the remnants of half-eaten gophers and mice all over the pasture—tiny feet and tails and little balls of fur, obviously the less tasty leavings of Vordor's unnatural snacks.

That had been almost a year ago, and Reb Chaim, distrustful of meat-eating bulls, had asked Gorig Gorovitch to keep Vordor away from his cows. "I don't want him teaching my ladies any mishegoss like that," he warned. But now, on this fine spring morning, the dew just drying from the grass, Reb Chaim froze in his tracks as he saw the hole in the fence and the bull Vordor chasing a gopher around the corner of his pasture, not a dozen meters from his precious Betzik.

"Hey!" yelled Reb Chaim, running at the charging bull and waving his hat in the air. "Get out of here, you meat-eating bull! Get out of my pasture!"

But Vordor was so intent in pursuit of his gopher that he paid no attention to Reb Chaim, and almost ran him down as he rushed by, hot on the heels of his prey. Reb Chaim ran to fetch Gorig Gorovitch, but by the time they arrived it was too late. Vordor had apparently caught the gopher and eaten it already. He was standing in the middle of Reb Chaim's pasture with a sated look of triumph on his face. Worse, he was staring at Betzik, who for her part wore a strange, coy look of shame.

Together the men chased Vordor back through

the hole in the fence, and then they roped Betzik and led her to a pen near Gorig Gorovitch's barn to be serviced, despite her protests, by Boris, a gentlemanly old black steer with none of Vordor's bad habits. Then they rebuilt the fence, and Gorig Gorovitch promised to keep Vordor on the other side of his property, well away from Reb Chaim's cows.

The months went by, and Reb Chaim forgot all about the incident. That is, until Betzik finally had her calf. It was a difficult birth, and required the help of four men to pull the calf by the ankles from its mother. The calf, when it finally emerged, seemed just fine except for one thing: she had a long forelock and a big white star on her forehead—just like Vordor's.

"Oy, veh is mir!" cried Reb Chaim, suddenly recalling Vordor's escapade in his pasture that spring. "Could that no-good meat-eating bull have been fooling around with my Betzik?"

Indeed, it seemed he had. For as the calf, whom Reb Chaim named Betzikala after her mother, grew up, she seemed to have all of the ornery bull's bad manners. When nursing, she often bit her mother's udders, and it got so bad that they had to feed her by hand. When Betzikala got old enough to be milked, she didn't stand patiently over the pail like her mother, but fussed and kicked and mooed in annoyance. When the herd was at pasture, Betzikala seemed not to care for the company of the other cows, who moved up and down the pasture in a group, but wandered off on her own, scratching the ground with her hooves and sniffing around. And if she had Vordor's mean streak, she also had his strength; she quickly outgrew her own mother, and as time passed it became clear that Betzikala gave more milk than any other cow on the farm.

Then the unthinkable happened. One afternoon Reb Chaim was again inspecting his herd when he saw Betzikala tearing around the pasture like she was possessed. She was chasing a mole! Desperate, Reb Chaim ran after her. "You, Betzikala, knock it off! Let that mole alone!" But before he could chase her off, Betzikala had cornered the mole and crushed it under her hoof. As he watched in horror, she devoured the poor rodent whole!

There was no doubt about it now. Betzikala, the daughter of his beloved Betzik, was the evil spawn of that meat-eating bull, Vordor. And then an even worse thought stabbed Reb Chaim's mind: Her milk could not be kosher. The laws of koshreth strictly forbid the mixing of meat and milk; and although Reb Chaim was always meticulous in keeping any utensils that had been used with meat far away from his milk, there could be no doubt that deep within the four stomachs of the cow, milk and meat had mixed! But even that wasn't the worst of it. For months now,

Reb Chaim had been mixing Betzikala's milk with that of the other cows and selling it to the Jews of the ghetto, and who knew how long she'd been eating meat on the sly? Everyone had drunk the milk, and now they had all sinned, unknowingly. And it was all Reb Chaim's fault!

Reb Chaim felt sick. If word got out that he'd been selling trayf milk to the ghettoites, his reputation and his business would be ruined forever. He lost no time in roping Betzikala, who seemed more than usually cranky, and locked her alone in a shed. Then he went directly to the home of my great-great-grandfather, Rabbi Shmul, as fast as his legs could carry him.

The rabbi and the dairyman sat down together, and in anguish Reb Chaim told Rabbi Shmul the whole story of the bull who ate gophers, the hole in the fence, and the calf with the star on her forehead who had just eaten a gopher before his very eyes.

"That's the craziest thing I've ever heard," said Rabbi Shmul. "Are you quite sure that's what you saw?"

"Rabbi, I know it's unbelievable, but it's true, I swear to you. And now what must I do? Must I kill Betzikala? It's been a bad year, Rabbi, and we can hardly afford to lose a cow. And even if I do take her to the shochet, will her meat be kosher? Who would eat the meat of a cow who eats meat? And what about the people who've drunk the milk from my dairy all these months? Has all the milk been defiled? Has the entire ghetto been contaminated? And what about me—what sin have I committed in allowing this to happen!"

This was a thorny problem indeed. Rabbi Shmul asked for a day to study the problem and think about it, and advised Reb Chaim to keep Betzikala isolated from the rest of the herd. He would have to discard her milk until a decision had been reached. Reb Chaim went him one better and had Gorig Gorovitch's son, Ivan, come over and milk Betzikala twice a day and carry the milk away in a sealed container. Probably Gorig Gorovitch's family drank that milk, he thought, but he didn't want to know about it, so he didn't ask.

At the end of the following day, Rabbi Shmul paid a call on Reb Chaim, who sat nervously fingering his teacup as the rabbi rendered his verdict.

"It is a very difficult problem," said my great-great-grandfather, "and I have had very little to guide me in my deliberations. There is nothing in the Talmud about cows who eat meat. Nothing like this has ever happened in the world before. So I have prayed to God—blessed be His holy name—to give me wisdom. And here is what I have decided.

"Several things are plain. The milk from this cow cannot be considered kosher and cannot be drunk by Jews. I say 'considered,' because there is no precedent for such a thing; maybe the milk is kosher, maybe not, but it is better to err on the side of safety. So, at the very least, you must keep this cow's milk separate from that of all your other cows, and on no account must you offer it for sale within the ghetto.

"On the other hand, the milk is probably safe for gentiles to drink. It may taste a little funny, but it is no more harmful to them than any of the other non-kosher dishes that are popular among them. Yet you yourself should not be the one to give it to them; it would be like encouraging them to sin, and it would bring shame upon you, even if they were to take it knowingly.

"Still, you may be forgiven for having supplied this milk to our people in the past, for you did so unwittingly and in good faith, and no atonement is necessary.

"Finally, it is not necessary to kill the cow. What is done is done, and cannot be undone, and nothing would be accomplished by killing the cow.

"That much is clear. But there are also several matters which are less clear, complicated matters which God has not given me the wisdom to understand. For one thing, even if this cow were killed by the shochet in a strictly kosher manner, the meat may or may not be edible to Jews. Surely the flesh of the gopher has gotten into the milk and ruined it; but that does not mean that the milk has gotten into the cow's own flesh. Every cow is made of flesh, and every cow is full of milk, yet we consider them kosher, do we not?

"On the other hand, can we really call this a cow? As you know, the laws of koshreth describe not only the preparation and combination of foods like meat and milk, they also dictate which animals may be used for eating meat and which may not. Pigs, of course, may not be eaten by Jews, because they are considered unclean. The law does not say why they are unclean, although it seems obvious just to look at them; but I think the reason may be that pigs will eat anything without discrimination—grains, meats, even filth. Now, a cow is an animal who eats grass and makes milk; but yours is an animal who eats rodents and makes trouble. So there is doubt whether this animal's unusual diet makes it acceptable for consumption by Jews, and again I think it best to err on the safe side.

"All things considered," Rabbi Shmul concluded, "I think you should sell the cow. Of course, you must not sell it to a Jew, which would be selling your tsouris to another. But you may sell it to a gentile, as long as you explain very clearly why it is being sold. Then your conscience can be clear."

And that, of course, is exactly what Reb Chaim did. In fact, he traded it to his neighbor, Gorig Gorovitch, for stud service on two of his regular, grass-eating cows, and both men thought it was a good deal. Reb Chaim was never again plagued by Vordor, the meat-eating bull. For after that Vordor stayed happily on his own far side of the pasture, where he spent his days in happy pursuit of gophers, moles, mice, and voles in the company of his bride—Betzikala, the meat-eating cow.

My Fellow Ghettoites

The following is taken directly from the "Gold Book," a sort of journal kept by my great-great-grandfather irregularly throughout his life. In the Gold Book, Rabbi Shmul jotted down his thoughts on many of the issues and events of his day, references to the Torah and the Talmud which he thought applicable, and the lessons he learned from them.

Among the entries in the Gold Book are also several character studies of individuals in the ghetto, portraits in words on which many of the stories in this book are based. I cannot say with certainty exactly why Grandpa Shmul wrote these little sketches. They don't seem to relate directly to the other subjects about which he wrote, and few of them have any obvious moral lesson. Perhaps he thought that someday a description of people as they were then would be of interest to people of future generations, when the life style of the people would have changed. But I rather think that he found in these individuals universal "types," with characteristics that apply more or less to each of us, of whatever generation, from whatever country. I believe that he was fascinated by these people just because they were people—"menshen," as they used to say in the shtetl—and I know he loved people.

The following was the last entry written in the Gold Book in my great-great-grandfather's hand (although notes and scribblings in various hands follow his on the book's dog-eared pages). By the time he wrote it, no doubt many of the individuals he described were dead. Yet he wrote about them as though they were still right next door, reinforcing my opinion that he regarded them as enduring "types." I give his descriptions of them just as he wrote them.

The shames of our shul is known by one and all as Shames Drayzuch. His real name is Yussel, but nobody ever calls him that. His nickname, Drayzuch, which means "turn yourself around," seems so appropriate to him because of his terrible clumsiness, that no one ever refers to him by any other name. In fact, he has borne that epithet patiently ever since he was a child.

Shames Drayzuch is a small, ascetic-looking man, with a short gray beard and steely blue eyes that give him a very distinguished appearance. When he stands upon the bima to lead our prayers, there is no doubt that he is truly a son of Abraham.

But whenever a task requires any kind of physical talent, we can expect him to botch it somehow, and we are seldom disappointed. For example, when Shames Drayzuch is asked to bring out extra chairs for visitors to the shul, he goes to his enormous storage closet, which contains all kinds of junk of timeless antiquity, and drags out the chairs that are the least broken. Infallibly he breaks at least one of them in the process. He keeps everything he ever had in that closet, no matter how old and derelict, and never throws anything away. If an item is broken (as most of the rubbish in the closet is), he swears he will repair it and avers that it would be a sin to throw it out. Never mind that in all these years he has never found the time to repair a single item from that huge inventory—nor that even if he did try to fix something, it surely would not stay fixed for long.

Despite his faults, Shames Drayzuch is loved by one and all in our shtetl because of his generosity, his willingness to listen to others' problems, and his eagerness to help people whenever he can. He never refuses a favor and never declines an appointment to any committee, even though he might already belong to several committees—some of which might meet at the same time. Perhaps that lends another meaning to his name, Drayzuch: to turn oneself to a task.

Our shames is always full of ideas that he is willing and anxious to share with the world. Whether the question is how to decorate a succah, how to care for an orphan, or whether gypsies can be married in the shul, Shames Drayzuch is ever ready with an answer. He is something of an idea man among us. Unfortunately, however, clever ideas are among of the few things that are never in short supply in our shtetl. Moreover, Shames Drayzuch's ideas are usually not well thought out, and are generally impractical—though they are certainly well intentioned. On the other hand, the shames is always willing to let his ideas be modified, or even to yield to the ideas of others. And so, over the years, I have had no better friend and helper than Shames Drayzuch.

In our shtetl there are many women who might be described as yentas [busybodies]. But among them is one whose God-given talent for invention outshines them all, so much so that most of us know her affectionately as Shmulke the Yenta. Shmulke is a short, roly-poly sort of woman. No one has ever been quite sure of her age; sometimes she looks like she might be fifty, sometimes she looks like a girl in her teens. But her tongue is surely of most venerable antiquity, for the tales it produces would put the prophets to shame. No matter what happens in our shtetl, Shmulke knows all about it, all the details; in fact, she often knows more about it than even the people involved. Her house is conveniently located at the entrance to our ghetto, where she is the first to observe who is coming in and who is going out, and when she is in her yard seeming to weed her onions or tend her flowers, she is really standing guard.

Moreover, whatever Shmulke cannot learn through gossip or snooping, she freely invents from her limitless imagination. For example, one day Chupa-Maya, the wife of Reb Hipsik, was seen sitting in the shul with her sheitel [wig] askew. The arbitrary rakish angle of the sheitel made it even less becoming than usual, but apparently Chupa-Maya had no idea that it had gone awry, and of course no one else had any idea why it might be so.

No one, that is, except Shmulke. That afternoon, Shmulke told her friends as they gathered at the well that Chupa-Maya had been told by a gypsy soothsayer that if she would place the sheitel atop the Torah, God would bless it, and the blessing would pass on to her every time she wore it—through her scalp, I suppose. So, according to Shmulke, Chupa-Maya had come to the shul early that morning and surreptitiously opened the ark and placed her sheitel on the Torah. Then suddenly Shames Drayzuch came into the shul, and Chupa-Maya, embarrassed, quickly slammed the ark shut, slapped the sheitel onto her head, and began tidying up as though she had come for just that purpose. And so the sheitel remained there, cocked to one side, for the rest of the day.

Everyone got a good laugh out of this story, not because they thought it was true, but because it was such an outrageously imaginative tale. Finally, however, one of the other women challenged Shmulke, saying, "You know that could not possibly be true. How can you make up such trash?"

But Shmulke was ready with a reply, as always. "Na, Mrs. Smarty-pants," she said, "if it's not true, perhaps you could tell us what *is* true? If you know it all, then tell us, tell us!"

At other times, however, Shmulke's stories are not so funny. Though they might be entertaining to her listeners, they have more than once brought misery to her victims. Like many of our people, Shmulke has very firm ideas about what is right and what is wrong, and she takes it as her own personal duty to see that everyone behaves rightly, according to her sense of it. I cannot entirely fault her for this. We are all responsible for each other; we are each our brothers' keeper, are we not? But Shmulke often takes this responsibility too far. When she is convinced that someone has misbehaved and brought shame to us, her imagination turns vindictive, and her tall tales become hurtful lies. There have been times, I must admit, when I have quite lost my temper with Shmulke and given her a piece of my own mind, and even more occasions on which I have had to step in and undo the damage that her stories have done.

One of the most difficult of our people for me to understand is Reb Vilhik, the shochet. Reb Vilhik never had any education to speak of; he was my student until the age of eight or so, when he quit his lessons and went to work with his father, who was our shochet before him.

All of our people love animals, and of the many restrictions the government places on our lives, the ban on pets is one of the hardest to bear. But Reb Vilhik, to the contrary, seems to have no feeling for animals whatsoever. He unceremoniously chops off their heads and casts them aside, one after another, in the most businesslike way. Perhaps his job demands this sort of callousness. It has been his duty to dispatch countless chickens, cows, and other animals over the years, and how could he do so if he fell in love with each of them first? Even the ritual prayer he says on behalf of each animal he slaughters seems hastily recited and without real devotion; but then again, he must have repeated that same prayer thousands of times by now.

On the other hand, it is perhaps Reb Vilhik's apparent lack of emotion that makes him one of the most practical-minded men among us. As I have said previously, our people come up with plenty of ideas, few of them good. So, for example, when we needed to build a footbridge over the Oloscev River, the little stream that flows through the shtetl, it was Reb Vilhik who drew up the plans and organized the work, he who bought the wood and nails, he who supervised the volunteers. That little bridge is still standing today, many years later. Reb Vilhik's attitude seems to be that when duty calls, a man must respond without fooling around. And surely no one can find fault with that.

We ghettoites are all very opinionated, but none more so than Reb Edgalla ben Rasha. No matter what anybody says, Reb Edgalla gets in the last word—whether he understands the subject or not. At a debate in the shul he will stamp his feet, bang his chair on the floor, and raise so much commotion in order to be heard that he frequently drowns out his own voice. It seems impossible for Reb Edgalla to agree with anyone, and it often happens that an opinion in whose defense he nearly suffered a heart attack on Monday will be the same one he attacks with all his might on Tuesday.

I remember a debate over koshreth that arose in the shul after Shabbes services several years ago. A group of men had formed and were discussing our dietary laws. Although they were not sure of the reasons for some of the rules, they all agreed that the rules seemed sensible, if only from the point of view of hygiene. But Reb Edgalla could not tolerate such harmony, and so he offered the dissenting opinion.

"It's kaibosh!" he said. "These old rules are from our days in the desert. They don't apply to today. For example, they don't take into account the way pigs are raised today; nowadays many farms keep their pigs clean and healthy, and most feed them the best grains and vegetables, not garbage. So why shouldn't we eat pork? And what about oysters? What did our ancestors know from oysters? They were out trapping them in the desert, I suppose? You can't hold on to a tradition that has no meaning anymore. Why venerate something just because it's old—does anyone want to doven to my old boot?" He actually took off his boot, set it before them, and then stomped around the room with one bare foot.

It was a most colorful diatribe, but I stayed out of it, because I knew Reb Edgalla well enough to realize that it would only encourage him. Besides, he knows no more about oysters than does the most sand-blown hermit, and like the rest of us he'd kept kosher all his long life. But he wouldn't give up until he had won; that was his way.

Finally, however, Reb Chaim, the dairyman, put an end to Reb Edgalla's rantings. "If our Torah says we must not eat chazzer, what would it hurt to obey? Aren't there enough other good foods to eat? Give it a rest, Edgalla! Give the word of God the benefit of the doubt, at least!"

Reb Edgalla stammered a few broken sentences, then sputtered and fell silent. It was one of the few times I have ever seen him stumped. From then on, I noticed, he chose his arguments a little more carefully, and never again took on the Haggadah or the Torah as an adversary.

If we have our share of opinionated people and people who feel it their duty to oversee the affairs of their neighbors, we also have people who would much rather keep to themselves and mind their own business. I am thinking in particular of Reb Aron ben Givenek, the most shy and timid man I have ever known. Reb Aron is very short, not more than a meter and a quarter tall, bald as a melon, and so skinny that you can almost see through him. He might weigh fifty kilos soaking wet, but I doubt it. His glasses are so thick and heavy that they are constantly sliding down his long nose, and his peculiar way of pushing them up with his thumb while turning away as though embarrassed is one of his most characteristic mannerisms.

I recall the time Reb Aron was asked to carry the Torah around the shul, an honor at which everyone eagerly takes his turn. But Reb Aron demurred. "I'd better not," he mumbled to Shames Drayzuch under his breath. "I'm afraid I'll drop it." And he refused thus to carry the Torah.

Amusing though that incident might be, there have been plenty of other times when Reb Aron's desperate shyness has been a great burden to him. Several years ago he finally realized that one of our shtetl's girls, Rachel-Chaina, was sweet on him. When they met outside the shul one Friday evening, Reb Aron was completely tongue-tied, and he actually began to turn purple. After that he disappeared for several days. No one could find either him or Rachel-Chaina, and nobody knew what to think (except Shmulke, of course). Then one Friday evening they both appeared together at the shul; they were now man and wife. It came out later that they had run off to Smolensk to be married; they knew it would be a great disappointment to their families, but it was the only way Rachel-Chaina could get him to marry her.

Finally, I must relate an amusing incident involving Reb Yahuda ben Shlomik, known among us as "the khokhem" [the wise one]. Part of Reb Yahuda's reputation comes from his voracious appetite for reading. He has read and remembers all of the classics, including the works of Pliny, Herodotus, and Shakespeare. Lately he is full of talk about the works of a new young writer, Dostoevsky is the name, I believe. Adding to Reb Yahuda's image is his stature. He is tall and well built, though not stout, and always stands erect, with his head held high. But he earned his agnomen by providing a surprising answer to a rather silly question from one member of our congregation. It's already an old story, but here it is:

Reb Khenka, a cobbler who is very poor because he never demands payment from his customers (most of whom are poorer than he is), was preparing his lunch one day in the little kitchen in the back of his shop. It had been a long time since anyone had paid him, and so all he had left to eat was a single piece of bread and just enough chicken shmaltz [fat] to spread on it. Grateful for even this, Reb Khenka sat down and began his meager meal, and carefully spread the shmaltz to the very edges of the piece of bread. But as he picked it up, he was startled by a gust of wind at his window, and the bread fell from his fingers and dropped to the floor.

To Reb Yahuda's amazement, however, the bread landed not face down, as he fully expected, but with the shmaltz side up, and it was still clean enough to eat. With great joy Reb Khenka shouted "Praise to God, blessed be his name! He and his angels must be watching over me, poor man though I am, for they have protected my lunch from harm!"

When he had finished his lunch, Reb Khenka came to my home to tell me of the unexpected blessing he had received. Reb Yahuda was there; we had been discussing Maimonides. Then Reb Khenka burst into the room and breathlessly told us the whole story of the bread that landed shmaltz-side up, ending with, "So you see, Rabbi, God loves even a poor man!"

But then Reb Yahuda spoke up. "Not so fast, Reb Khenka," he said with a facetious twinkle in his eye. "Rabbi Shmul and I have been studying Maimonides, and I believe you are mistaken. This is not God's doing at all. In fact, it is your own fault. For it was you who put the shmaltz on the wrong side of the bread."

People like these make our life what it is—entertaining, eventful, and full to the back teeth with the joys and sorrows that make human beings out of us. Whatever their faults, I am happy to be among them, and grateful that I have this opportunity to serve as their rabbi.

The Salesman's Donation

In the ghettos of Russia in the time of the czars, as in many Jewish households today, it was strictly forbidden to work on the Shabbes—the time from sunset on Friday to sunset on Saturday. This injunction applied not only to going to one's job or practicing one's profession; especially among the more orthodox ghettoites, such activities as riding on a horse or in a wagon, cleaning, cooking, or even lighting a fire were avoided from sunset on Friday to sunset on Saturday. Instead, pious Jews devoted themselves to prayer, study, and what would today be called "quality time" with their families.

Of course, the world didn't stop because of the calendar. No matter what day it is, dust accumulates under the furniture, and shoes track mud across the floor; people need to eat, and the garbage needs to be carried out. Work waits for no one. To help them get through the Shabbes without starving to death or having dirt pile up around their ankles, those ghettoites who could afford to do so hired help from among the village Christians. Such a helper was known as a "Shabbes Goy" (the epithet being without the negative connotation which modern readers might assume). This arrangement was a boon not only to the Jews, who could still eat well in a clean home and enjoy a much-deserved day off; it also served as a form of social welfare. In those days, when preventive medicine was not what it is today, minor diseases like influenza would each year leave a few widows in every village. Generally these unfortunate women had no saleable skills other than domestic ones, and often these were quite good (of course, this was in the days before frozen dinners and washing machines were invented). Faced with having to support themselves and their children in the absence of their husbands, they were all too happy to be able to earn a little extra money in addition to what they could get from taking in laundry and such. They were willing, if only for a day, to lay aside the prejudices that usually separated Jew from gentile—and in this way the custom of the Shabbes Goy may have even helped to break down some of those barriers.

All of the better households in the ghetto of Orsha employed Shabbes Goyim—including the household of Shames Drayzuch and his wife, Chupa-Ala. Their helper was a young widow named Nadja, whose husband had been taken by an outbreak of influenza that had left an unusual number of mourners in both the village and the ghetto. Nadja had no children, which was fortunate because it made it more likely that she might someday remarry, and also because Nadja didn't have any particular skills, either, and couldn't have supported children if she had any. She was really a pretty mediocre housekeeper, as the Drayzuch family found. When she swept or did laundry, she would get about eighty percent of the dirt; when she cooked she would burn about ten percent of the food.

Those are not such bad averages, perhaps, but they were well below what Chupa-Ala expected of herself; nevertheless, the shames' wife felt kindly toward the poor young widow and overlooked her shortcomings. Secretly she thought that Nadja might not be quite right in the head—not seriously meshuggah, just a little bit soft—and this made her even more fond of the girl. She taught her how to prepare a few of the family's favorite meals and showed her how she liked the house kept. Nadja wasn't too quick on the uptake, but she was willing and good-hearted enough, and Chupa-Ala would often give her a few kopeks extra and send her home with some leftovers to tide her over during the week. In this way a warm friendship built up between the Drayzuch family and their helper. Until one week in April, when things began to turn up missing.

At first Chupa-Ala didn't notice anything was missing. Certainly Shames Drayzuch didn't notice; he could never remember where he'd left anything, anyway. But his wife ran a tight ship, and if a spoon was out of place or even the tiniest piece of costume jewelry was gone, she'd have noticed it right away. But it wasn't anything like that. It was little things, useless junk, really, that she finally missed—and that's what made it so strange. One day she had half a bottle of milk left over, and remembered that she had once stashed a large cork in a box of things at the back of the highest kitchen shelf. (Chupa-Ala remembered things like that.) But when she went to look, there was no cork. The shames' wife was frustrated—not by the absence of the cork, but because she thought her memory was playing tricks on her; she felt *sure* she had hidden a cork there.

Then, a week later, she lost a button from her Shabbes dress, the one she wore to the shul every week. The dress, which she had made herself, had very pretty buttons made of malachite. Chupa-Ala was not alarmed, however, because when she made the dress she had been clever enough to buy an extra button and squirrel it away in the back of her sewing drawer, ready against just such an emergency. But when she opened the drawer and rummaged around in the back of it, there was no button to be found. Not only that, but an old rusty thimble that had once belonged to her great-aunt Sophia was also missing. And she knew, she absolutely *knew*, that those items had been in that drawer not a week before, for she had seen them there with her very own eyes. Now they were gone.

There were three possibilities. For one, she might be dreaming all this. Chupa-Ala stood up and flapped her arms vigorously up and down; but no, she was not dreaming, or she would have flown away. She might have lost her mind, she thought, so she took up a pen and wrote on a scrap of paper her name, her birthdate, her husband's name, the present date, and the name of the czar; these she checked against entries in her family scrapbook and on the calendar in the kitchen, and found herself to be quite sane. Finally she thought perhaps the cork, button, and thimble might have been taken by a mouse, and she shuddered at the very thought of vermin in her house. But after searching high and low she was unable to find any of the tiny black cylinders that are the calling cards of the household rodent. In the end she was stumped. She was relieved to find herself awake, competent, and free of pestilence, but she couldn't imagine where on earth these little things might have gotten to.

The following Friday night, however, she found out. She and her husband had just returned from the shul, where she had sat through an unusually long, tedious lecture by him, and she wasn't in the mood for talking. Instead she shuffled around the house, trying to keep her hands busy without really working, just sort of tidying things up a little bit. When she went into the kitchen she noticed that Nadja, who had been there cleaning while they were at the shul, had left her sweater. "That girl would forget her ears…" she thought to herself as she picked up the sweater to put it away until the morrow. And as she did so, from its inverted pocket fell the three things the shames' wife least expected to see at that moment: a large cork, a malachite button, and a rusty old thimble that had once belonged to her great-aunt Sophia.

So there it was. Chupa-Ala didn't want to believe it, but the evidence was incontrovertible that Nadja—poor Nadja, dear sweet soft-headed Nadja—had been pilfering her things. But why in the world would anyone steal such trash, things that had no real value at all, things that, except for the button, weren't even pretty to look at? It was an enigma wrapped in a riddle, and Chupa-Ala had no answer for it, so she decided to keep her discovery to herself and be on the lookout for anything else that might turn up missing.

Several weeks went by without further incident. Nadja showed up every Friday promptly at three in the afternoon, all smiles and hugs and ready to go to work. She cleaned the house and heated up the meals. Unfortunately, she managed to shrink the shames' favorite woolen shirt and overheat the kreplach until they were sodden wads of glue; but Chupa-Ala didn't miss any more household items, and after a while she forgot all about the affair.

Then one sunny Friday morning a traveling shoe salesman came into the ghetto. Most everyone knew Yonkel Khashky already; three or four times a year he would show up, driving his rickety old wagon through the ghetto singing, "Shoes for you! Shoes of all sizes! Shoes of all kinds! Shoes for sale!" accompanied by the merry tinkle of little bells tied to his horse's bridle. Unlike most salesmen, Yonkel Khashky didn't carry a full stock of goods with him. It would have been impossible to carry all the different styles of shoes he had to offer, in all the different sizes people might need. Instead he carried a large bag full of samples, one left shoe in each style, and he would stop at all the cobblers' shops, mercantile stores, and public squares, taking orders that would be shipped directly from the factory in Smolensk for which he worked.

All day long the ghettoites heard Yonkel Khashky's song and bells drifting up and down the ghetto alleys, and then, as was his custom, he stopped at the shul at about three o'clock, where he knew he would find Shames Drayzuch preparing for the evening service. Now, the salesman wasn't a particularly religious man. In fact, he wasn't even a faintly religious man. But over the years he had struck up a friendship with the shames, and he was sure that the good-hearted Drayzuch would offer him a place to stay for a couple nights during the shabbes.

"Good afternoon, Shames," said the salesman obsequiously, bowing and removing his hat as he entered the shul. "And a lovely afternoon it is, praise be to God."

"Hello to you, Yonkel Khashky," said the shames over his shoulder as he struggled to untangle two chairs that had somehow become tangled together while he was moving them across the room. When he had freed the chairs from each other, and himself from them, he at last looked at his guest. "And how are sales today?"

"Nu," said Yonkel Khashky, "just so-so. In the fall, you know, sales are good, with the cold weather coming. But now, in the spring, who needs shoes?"

"True enough," said the shames. "And will you be staying the night?"

"God willing I awake in the morning," quipped the salesman, "and your wife willing that I take your extra room."

"Of course," said Shames Drayzuch, "of course." It almost went without saying that the salesman would spend the night in the shames' spare bedroom, as he always did whenever he found himself in Orsha on the sabbath. "And I hope you'll join us for our service this evening?"

"Indeed, I wouldn't miss it," said the salesman politely; though if the truth were known he'd rather be just about anywhere else. Still, it was a small price to pay for a room for the weekend.

Reb Yonkel helped Shames Drayzuch finish setting up the chairs, and when they were done the two of them climbed into Yonkel Khashky's wagon and rode off to the shames' house, where, as usual, the salesman unhitched his horse at put it in the barn. He left his bag of samples by the front door, then went to the back bedroom to freshen up. Then, after a light supper prepared by Chupa-Ala with help from Nadja, the salesman, the shames, and Chupa-Ala went together to the shul.

The following day was Saturday, the other half of

the Shabbes, and no one thought of work but Nadja, who waited on the shames and his guest in the morning and afternoon and even stayed on throughout the evening because there was company. Therefore it was not until the following morning, Sunday, when Yonkel Khashky had packed his grip, hitched his horse to his rickety old wagon, and bid a fond farewell to his friend the shames that, turning to go, he suddenly noticed that his bag of left-footed shoe samples was not where he had left it by the door.

"Oh," said the shames, "I'm sure our Nadja has put it out of the way. Nadja!" he called, and the girl came running. "Have you seen Reb Yonkel's sack of samples that was here by the door on Friday night?"

"Why, no, rebbe," said Nadja, "I never saw any sack of samples by the door Friday night."

But Chupa-Ala, who stood by watching, wasn't convinced. She saw how Nadja shifted uneasily from one foot to the other, and noticed how the girl twisted her knuckles together beneath her apron. And of course she remembered the cork, the malachite button, and the rusty thimble from her great-aunt Sophia. She'd been expecting something like this.

But still Chupa-Ala said nothing. She couldn't be sure, of course; and she didn't want to embarrass the girl in front of everybody. Instead she kept her own counsel and watched helplessly as

The Salesman's Donation

her husband and Yonkel Khashky turned the house upside down looking for the missing samples. Finally, on the back porch, they found Reb Yonkel's sample bag—but nearly all of the shoes were gone.

The shames nearly panicked, and the shoe salesman was furious. Where could the sample shoes have gone, they all wondered? Who would steal a bunch of odd-sized, mismatched shoes, anyway? Were there rats in the house? Perish the thought! Or were they all dreaming—or mad?

In confusion, anger, and alarm, Shames Drayzuch, Chupa-Ala, and Yonkel Khashky made their way to the home of my great-great-grandfather, Rabbi Shmul, to report the missing shoes. They found the rabbi taking tea and mandelbrot with his friend, Dr. Shatsky, and of course they were invited to join them. When Grandpa asked the troubled shames to unburden himself, he told him all about the empty sack of left-footed shoes.

Throughout the brief narrative, Rabbi Shmul sat silent, the look on his face growing more concerned with every detail. But it was Dr. Shatsky, who had been listening even more closely and becoming more and more agitated as the tale progressed, who finally broke in.

"Friends, I think I can shed some light on this little problem," he said. "I don't think you're dreaming, and I know you're not mad. And God forbid you should have rats in your house—which you don't, I'm sure. But I'm sorry to tell you that you may have a thief under your roof. Your Shabbes Goy, Nadja."

Shames Drayzuch gasped and Reb Yonkel shouted "A-ha!" But Chupa-Ala had known it was coming, and cast her gaze sadly into her lap.

"I know of your Nadja," the doctor continued. "In fact, Dr. Smirnov, the Christian doctor, and I were discussing her case just the other day. What I'm going to tell you is confidential, and I wouldn't tell you at all except that I think you must know, so promise that you won't repeat it to anyone. Nadja is not dishonest; she's sick. Dr. Smirnov thinks she has a psychological disorder known as kleptomania—that is, an uncontrollable urge to take what does not belong to her. It isn't stealing; a kleptomaniac doesn't covet the wealth of others. He or she just sees something—anything, whether it has any value or not—and has an uncontrollable urge to take it. It could be something valuable, like jewelry; or it could be something as worthless as a button." Here Chupa-Ala began to cry quietly. "In this case, it seems it was a bag of odd shoes. It doesn't matter that they were all left shoes of various sizes. She found them, and she had to have them, and that was it. Or so I think."

"Oh, my…" said Shames Drayzuch. "So what can we do? How do you help a person like that?"

"And how will I get my samples back?" broke in

The Salesman's Donation

Reb Yonkel.

"Science has only just recently recognized kleptomania as a disease," said Dr. Shatsky, "and I'm not sure you can help her at all. Dr. Smirnov is doing what he can, but who knows if he'll be successful? As for your samples," he continued, addressing the angry salesman, "you might never see them again. A person with this disease might also hide what she steals so that no one will ever find it. Or she may have destroyed the shoes. I really don't know. Anyway, chances are that if you ask her about the shoes, she'll tell you nothing; most likely she won't even remember ever having seen them."

With that advice—and a cup of tea and a slice of Rebbitsin Helga's mandelbrot to wash it down—the trio thanked the doctor and took their leave. Shames Drayzuch and his wife were deeply saddened. They were not too worried about the shoes, but they were heartbroken to hear the news about their dear Nadja. Yonkel Khashky, on the other hand, hadn't forgotten about a single left-footed slipper, and he was fuming with impotent rage.

But as they turned the corner, they saw something that froze them all in their tracks. They stood at the entrance to what was known as "widows' square," a sort of hollow spot in a neighborhood where there lived unusual number of women who had been widowed by a plague of diphtheria several years ago. And there, to their utter amazement, they saw perhaps a dozen old women waddling across the square wearing ratty old sandals on their right feet, and Yonkel Khashky's shiny new samples on the left!

It was a sight to make you crosseyed. There was an old lady wearing a babushka and a drab gray apron wearing one bright-red evening slipper; there was another mournful-looking woman, her house dress patched with flour sacks and mattress ticking, wearing a shiny patent-leather pump, its heel broken off to make it even with her old, worn, rope-soled shoe. And so on and so on, and all the women limping around unevenly like drunken wind-up dolls.

Immediately all three of them realized what had happened. Nadja must have found the shoes and compulsively taken them; then, not knowing what to do with them, she must have "hidden" them in plain sight by distributing them among the other widows of Orsha and its ghetto. Immediately they turned back to tell the rabbi and the doctor what they had seen.

Even Yonkel Khashky was moved by the sight. "Those poor women!" he said to Rabbi Shmul. "Imagine being in such dire straits that it's better to have one good shoe and one bad one than to have a matched pair!" Obviously, there was no chance of getting his samples back; he wouldn't have had the heart for it, anyway. Instead, to everyone's surprise, he promised to return the next week with right-footed mates for all the left-footed samples, and he asked Rabbi Shmul to distribute them to the appropriate wearers.

Thus the irreligious salesman made his first donation to the ghetto's poor—and, for all we know, his only donation. On Dr. Shatsky's advice, the shames and his wife said nothing about the shoes to their helper, Nadja, who wouldn't have known what they were talking about anyway. Nor did they fire her, as they might have been justified in doing. Instead they kept a close eye on her as she left the house at the end of the shabbes, and she remained with them for several more years, until at last she remarried and the shames and his wife found a new Shabbes helper.

For Rabbi Shmul the incident of the stolen shoes and the salesman's donation was a lesson. It was proof again that God—blessed be His holy name—works in unconventional ways. He had taken a poor young widow with a mental problem and a salesman with no thought but to sell, and put them together to provide shoes for the widows of Orsha. Sometimes, it seems, even theft can turn into a mitzvah.

Frum

Frum is the Yiddish word for "religious," but it goes way beyond its mild English equivalent. Frum means "devoted" in the fullest sense, devoutly adherent to every letter of the law in all matters of religion, and of life as well.

   Nearly all the people living in the ghetto of Orsha in my great-great-grandfather's time practiced Judaism as strictly as possible. They didn't just go to the shul to recite their prayers on Friday nights, on Saturdays, and on holidays—although they certainly did all that. But they also let their very lives be guided by the principles of their faith. This included, for example, keeping strictly to the dietary laws of koshreth, being obedient to their parents and dutiful to their children, keeping their homes neat as a pin, and so on. Anything that conflicted with this devout piety—any casual slip of the hand or tongue, any indiscretion however minor or unintended—was a blemish truly to be regretted.

No doubt about it, the people of Orsha deserved the epithet "Fummer Yiddineh," which means so much more than "pious Jews." Nevertheless, every year when Yom Kippur came around, all the adult men and women could be found at the shul, beating their breasts and praying for forgiveness of their sins—not only sins they knew they had committed, but also sins they might have committed unwittingly, and even the sins of others, which were also, in the peculiar logic of Judaism, their responsibility.

One of the best times to be frum is during Pesach, the week-long festival that celebrates the Jews' liberation from bondage in Egypt. It is a time to dress one's best, to meet and celebrate with family and friends, and to take joy and pride in our ancestors' long and difficult history of frummigkeit, if I may coin such a word.

It was the eve of Pesach in the ghetto, and Yussel Drayzuch, the shames of the shul, was getting dressed for the celebration. He felt light and buoyantly happy as he looked forward to the holidays. How warm and wonderful it would be to celebrate the seder with his family; how sweet it would be to hear his little son, Ezek, ask the kashas, the four questions that probe the history of Jewish people and traditions. In preparation for the holiday, the shames' household had been cleaned from top to bottom by his wife, Chupa-Ala. As custom demanded, she had removed every last trace of chometz—things not kosher for Passover, especially leavened foods like bread—and now the shames' heart felt as clean and pure as his house.

Humming an old favorite song under his breath, the shames pulled on his newest black coat and adjusted it on his shoulders. He inspected it carefully; not too bad, he thought. The cuffs had barely become shiny yet, and he carefully brushed away a few specks of lint from the sleeves. Then he reached up to the very highest shelf of the closet, where he hoped to find among the hats the new yarmulke Chupa-Ala had made for him especially for this Pesach. It was a beautiful thing, a holiday yarmulke of heavy white silk and elaborate gold embroidery, all stitched by the loving hand of his wife.

But as the shames' fingers groped in the darkness, they found only the brims of hats of wool and cotton and beaver; but no yarmulke could he feel. Where can it have gone, he wondered? It was here just yesterday. He rummaged around some more, but his fingers found only hats—hats, hats, and more hats. Why in the world should anyone have so many hats when he only had one head, he thought?

Then his fingers found something that was not a hat; something hard and coarse, something stiff and crumbly. He pulled it down and looked at it, and his heart stood still. It was a crust of bread—chometz—in his house on the very eve of Pesach!

"Gevalt!" he shouted at the top of his lungs, and he immediately began yelling for his wife. "Chupa-Ala! Come here at once! Our house is not clean! I've found…chometz!"

To anyone who is not a Jew, and perhaps even to some modern Jews, it might be hard to understand what a disaster this simple crust of bread was to the shames. Just throw it out, one might say, and be sure to get all the crumbs if it bothers you so much. It's only a crust of bread.

But to Shames Drayzuch, that dried-up piece of flour and yeast was both a catastrophe and a conundrum. It had polluted his house, but where had it come from? And how had it gotten up onto the top shelf of the closet? Had his little son, Ezek, thrown it up there to hide it for later? Had the cat somehow dragged it up there? Or a mouse? God forbid there should be vermin in the house! And how had his wife not found it there during her meticulous cleaning? How many years had it lain there unsuspected and undiscovered; how many Pesachim had been defiled by this evil crust without his even suspecting it? It may have looked like an ordinary crust of bread to you, but to the shames it looked like Beelzebub, and he would have been no less upset to have found the devil himself in his closet. What kind of a frummer Yid—and a shames, no less—would have chometz in his closet at Pesach?

"Chupa-Ala! Wife! Where are you! There's... there's...*chometz* in our house!"

"What is it?" said Chupa-Ala as she came running to his call. "What in the world are you carrying on about? Are you looking for your yarmulke? Here, I put it on your dresser for you, it's right here."

"Woman, don't you see?" cried the shames, holding the crust at arm's length between his fingertips, as though it would infect him. "Look what I found in the closet: a crust of bread—chometz, I tell you—in our house at Pesach!"

"Oh, dear," she said, trying to mollify him. "Where did that come from? Give it to me, and I'll get rid of it right away."

"Right away, indeed!" raved the shames. "What is it doing here in the first place? How could you have been so careless as to leave this...this... *thing* in our house? And how long has your carelessness been going on—a year, two, three? Or more? Yes, here, take it, get rid of it; right away, indeed! Right away yesterday; right away a week ago; right away last year, and the year before that, and the year before that!"

Chupa-Ala took the crust from her husband and carried it out, apologizing all the while. The shames found his yarmulke on the dresser where his wife had left it for him, in plain sight, and put it on. But his mind was not at ease. He had sinned—she had sinned—no, they both had sinned, and they must atone for it before the Pesach celebrations began.

"Wife," he called, "get your coat. We must go to see the rabbi."

Rabbi Shmul was taking tea and studying the Talmud when Shames Drayzuch and his wife knocked at the door and came in. The shames was sputtering and fuming, red in the face, and his wife stood meekly behind him, her hands fumbling nervously behind her shawl.

"Rabbi, we have a problem," said the shames. "We have discovered chometz in our house—in the closet, to be precise. I found this morning an old crust of bread."

Rabbi Shmul looked concerned, but not shocked as the shames had expected, and so he continued. "My wife assured me that our house was perfectly clean for Pesach. But apparently it was not. And I don't know how many years she, in her negligence, has overlooked this defilement, how many Pesachim have been ruined by her carelessness. What must we do, Rabbi, to atone for her oversight, to make up for this...this...this...."

"Woah!" said my great-great-grandfather, holding up his hands. "Stop the cart and back up a bit. Why don't you come in and sit down, and tell me what this is all about."

Reb Drayzuch and Chupa-Ala took off their coats, and Rabbi Shmul poured them some tea while the shames explained in painstaking detail the exact sequence of events that had led him to discover the crust in the closet. Then he described the crust itself, its size, its weight, its color, its texture; and finally he started in again blaming his wife for allowing their house to be improperly cleaned for Pesach.

"Okay, okay," Rabbi Shmul said at last, "I get the idea. Just calm down a little bit and look at this rationally. Maybe it's not so bad as all that, if the crust was truly overlooked. As you know, shames, there's a difference between a sin committed intentionally and an honest mistake.

"In fact," he continued, thumbing through the Talmud, "I was just reading a story about exactly that difference. Here," he said, stopping at a page and laying the book open on the table. "Let me explain. Here's a story about a roofer who was repairing the roof of a man's house. He was up there hammering and hammering, nailing and nailing, when all of a sudden—*crash*—the roof caved in. He fell right through the attic and landed on top of the wife of the man who owned the house, and as she fell to the ground her dress flew up, exposing her privates. So right there, on the spur of the moment, the roofer made love to her. Has he committed a sin? And if so, how bad a sin?

"So, all right, it's not the most convincing story in the world. These Talmudists were scholars, very wise men, but not necessarily the best storytellers. But the story has a point, and the point is that although the roofer sinned, it was not a sin he had planned beforehand and committed maliciously. No, it was quite an accident—at first, anyway—and the roofer is less to blame than someone who had, say, broken into the house for the purpose of violating the woman.

"On the other hand, when a sin is premeditated and committed on purpose, it is another matter entirely," the rabbi went on, flipping to another page. "Here's another story about a young student of a famous rabbi who hid himself under the rabbi's bed one night in order to spy on the rabbi and his wife. That night, while the rabbi and his wife were making love, the student kept getting hit on the head by the bouncing mattress, until finally he cried out 'Ow!' So then the rabbi dragged him out from under the bed and gave him a good what-for standing right there in his altogether. 'But, rabbi,' said the student, 'today in class you spoke of the difference between sins that are intended and those that are accidental, and I did not understand. So I wanted to see if I could observe the difference.' 'You fool,' said the rabbi, 'your sin is that you snuck into my house—a very grave sin, indeed!'

"Well, maybe not the best story ever written, but you get the point. Everyone sins, and everyone makes mistakes—even a shames' wife—even a shames—why, even a rabbi. Finding this little bit of chometz in your house is not really so bad at all. In fact, it isn't even really a sin; it's a mistake, that's all, and there's no need to atone for a simple mistake. And your dear wife is hardly to blame. She cleaned the house from top to bottom, worked her fingers to the bone. So she missed one little crust? Who would think to look for a crust of bread in a clothes closet?"

He paused and smiled at Chupa-Ala, who beamed her vindication back at him. "A clever woman she surely is, a real heilige Veib and a careful housekeeper, as we both know. But Madame Blavatsky she is not," he added, referring to the spiritualist who had been so much in the news of late, "so how should she know there's bread in the closet?" Chupa-Ala smiled.

"You've removed the offending crust already, no doubt?" Grandpa asked Chupa-Ala, and she nodded her assent. "Good," he said, rising from his chair and closing the Talmud. "Then let us go to the shul; the sun has nearly set."

Sherlock Shmul

In the old days of the ghettos of Russia in the time of the czars, priests and rabbis were called upon to solve all sorts of problems for the people. Not only spiritual, ethical, and moral dilemmas, though these were the most common; but also political debates, domestic disputes, unpaid debts, and even crimes from the most petty to the most heinous were brought to them when no other authority was able to help. The people were awed by the prescience of their holy men, who seemed to know all, past, present, and future. It seemed as if they were so close to God that they heard the secrets that fell from His lips while He was about other business. And besides, they would never go to the police if they could possibly avoid it; to do so could only bring more problems on top of the old ones.

Crime was not common in those days, certainly not like it is today. Most of what passed for "crime" was really petty squabbles that were elevated to criminal status simply because there was nothing worse to get upset about. Like the time Reb Histek's running-jumping rooster defied the property rights of the neighbors by jumping over the fence. It's a fact of human nature that things get blown out of all proportion when there is nothing else to complain about.

But occasionally—very occasionally—serious crimes were committed. It so happened that one morning a Russian Orthodox grocer in Orsha was found robbed and murdered in his shop. No one witnessed the crime in progress; it was only some hours later that a villager entered, found the awful scene, and called the police. The store had been ransacked, shelves turned over, potatoes and beets were all over the floor, and the cash drawer had been emptied. Upon closer scrutiny, the police discovered that all that was missing was the cash and an unknown number of bottles of liquor. The worst, however, was what had happened to the poor shopkeeper. His throat had been slit from ear to ear, and his body left lying in a crimson pool of his own blood. The only evidence that could be found was a single bloody footprint heading out the door.

For a week the police "investigated" the crime. That is to say, they enlisted the help of the Cossacks and arrested, questioned, and roughed up nearly a hundred people, chosen more or less at random. But no matter whom they rounded up, interrogated, threatened, or slapped across the face, they could learn nothing that might help them find the murderer.

Captain Magirkik of the police was at a loss. By the end of the week he had to admit that the investigation was going nowhere, and he, for one, was smart enough to see that it wouldn't go anywhere, either. He was just about at the end of his rope. Then it occurred to him to consult his old friend, Rabbi Shmul. He and the rabbi had often helped each other solve their respective problems, as when the ghettoites had trouble with the tax collector, or when a fugitive had taken refuge among the Jews. Captain Magirkik had come to not only trust the rabbi, but to admire his wisdom and insight. Indeed, he was under the same spell of awe as almost everyone else, and like everyone else, when he was stumped he turned to the rabbi for help.

So one afternoon the captain paid a call on my great-great-grandfather and explained the affair to him over a pot of tea and several slices of mandelbrot provided by Helga, the rebbitsin.

"So that's how it stands, Rabbi," he said in conclusion. "We have nothing to go on, and I can't go on arresting everybody in Orsha and letting the Cossacks have their way with them. They enjoy their work too much, those brutes, and the more frustrated they get, the more they abuse the suspects. I'm ready to find a scapegoat and call the whole thing off. Unless you have a suggestion?"

Rabbi Shmul said nothing. With his chin resting on his chest, the lower half of his face buried in his beard, he looked as if he might be asleep. Finally, however, he opened his eyes and sat up straight.

"Captain, this is truly a difficult case. But it is also a very serious one, and the true murderer must be found, not just a scapegoat, before he has a chance to harm anyone else. You have told me what you know, which as you admit is little. Now let me ask you a few questions. If you can find answers to them, you may also find your man.

"You have told me that all that was stolen was some cash and some liquor. I would surely like to know what kind of liquor. Was it local vodka? Or was it expensive imported liquor—perhaps some cognac from France, or some Bourbon from America? Maybe some arak from Turkey or some ouzo from Greece?"

"What possible difference could that make?" protested the captain. "Is a thief no less a thief who steals eggs rather than hens?"

"We'll see when we find out," said the rabbi. "It may be very important, or it may not. Please take an inventory of what remains in the store, and let me know what is missing."

The captain seemed puzzled, but he promised to do as the rabbi asked.

"I am also very interested in the wound on the poor grocer's throat," Rabbi Shmul continued with a shudder. "Forgive my indelicacy, but have you noticed whether the wound was deeper on either side, the left or the right?"

"I couldn't say, Rabbi," confessed the police captain. "He was so covered with blood I didn't notice. Anyway, what does it matter? It killed him equally on both sides, didn't it? But I'll check. We sent the body straight to the undertaker; he might know."

"Good," said Rabbi Shmul. "The other thing that concerns me," he continued, "is the footprint you found. Can you describe it in more detail? Is it from the right shoe, or the left?"

"Now, Rabbi, who cares whether it was the right shoe or the left? The murderer came on two feet in any case. But if you insist, I'll find out."

"Please do," said the rabbi. "And while you're at it, please look most carefully at the print and see if there are any unusual markings. Be very careful to examine the area near the ball of the foot, and see if it looks any different from the rest of the print."

Again Captain Magirkik promised to find out, though he protested that he couldn't see why it would make any difference.

"Don't worry about the difference," said my great-great-grandfather, smiling reassuringly and rising from his chair. "You bring me the answers to these questions, and we'll see if they don't lead to the murderer."

Captain Magirkik left shaking his head, not understanding how these picky details would be of any help. But he promised to find the answers and return the next day.

The following afternoon, Captain Magirkik returned as promised, this time with a glimmer of hope in his eyes.

"I have your answers, Rabbi," he announced as Rabbi Shmul ushered him in and poured him a cup of tea. "But I still don't know how they'll help."

"Never mind," said Rabbi Shmul. "What can you tell me?"

"Well, first I looked at the store's inventory, as you said, and I was surprised to find that the shelves were still full of expensive imported spirits. But there was not a drop of vodka to be found anywhere on the premises. Now, what do you make of that, Rabbi? What kind of fool would steal only cheap vodka and leave expensive cognac behind?"

"A very poor fool," Rabbi Shmul answered immediately. "One who is used to drinking only vodka, one who wouldn't know what to do with a bottle of cognac if he found it on his doorstep."

Captain Magirkik furrowed his brow. "As you say, Rabbi; but I don't see how you can infer...."

"Never mind," interrupted Rabbi Shmul. "Please go on, and we'll see if I am right. Did you speak with the undertaker?"

"I did," said the captain. "He told me that in fact the wound was very much deeper on the left side than on the right. The right side, he said, was barely scraped; but the left side was cut clean through, almost to the bone."

"Now, that is interesting," said Rabbi Shmul. "It is a very important clue, and greatly narrows our field of suspects. This murderer was undoubtedly left-handed. A left-handed man, standing behind the victim, would have begun his cut on the right side, pulling toward the left, and the wound would naturally get deeper as it went."

Magirkik was stunned. "Why, that may very well be. But there are lots of lefties in Orsha."

"What about the footprint?" Rabbi Shmul went on, ignoring the captain's protest.

"I examined it myself," said the captain, "as soon as I left here yesterday. And just as you said, there appeared to be some unevenness to the print, a roundish mark, a kind of shadow, about halfway up the sole, right about where the ball of the foot would be. And it was the right foot."

"Yes," said the rabbi, squinting off into the distance and smiling vaguely, "just as I suspected. The murderer has a hole in the sole of his shoe, the right shoe. When you told me about the wound, I knew that it must be the right shoe that left the print. As the victim collapsed into the free right arm of the left-handed murderer, it would naturally be the right shoe that would step in the pool of blood.

"As to the hole, it is not unusual, of course, to have a hole in one's shoe." To prove his point, he lifted his foot and showed the captain the hole under the ball of his foot. "Many of us wear our shoes until we wear them out. But these are not the shoes I wear when I go out; I have a better pair for that. And as you'll recall, it rained the night before the murder. It proves my point that the murderer is a poor man—indeed, it seems, a very poor man, a man so poor that he had no other shoes to wear on a wet day."

The police captain was astonished. "This is amazing, Rabbi! So it is your opinion that our murderer is a poor man, a left-handed man, a man who drinks only vodka?"

"Just so," said Rabbi Shmul with a satisfied smile.

"But just a minute," said the captain. "There must be a hundred poor left-handed people who drink only vodka. Even if all this is true, how can we find this needle in the haystack?"

Rabbi Shmul smiled broadly now. "Yes, captain, there are many poor left-handed vodka-drinkers in the village. But this one is different: this one is not poor anymore. He's been poor a long time, of that I am certain; but as of last week he has become rich beyond his wildest dreams. And that is how we will find him."

Captain Magirkik sat on the edge of his chair as he listened to Rabbi Shmul's instructions. "First you must make the rounds of all the cobblers in Orsha and find out which of them has been given a right shoe for resoling. When you find it, you may check for bloodstains, and if they are present you will know it is the murderer's shoe. Perhaps the cobbler will even be able to identify him for you; at least he will be able to give you a description.

"At the same time, you may canvas the pubs and see whether there has been any poor man with money to burn; perhaps he bought a round of drinks for his friends, or for the entire house—a round of vodka, of course. If so, perhaps the bartender can corroborate the cobbler's evidence.

"Meanwhile, you and your men may keep an eye out for a barefoot man. There won't be many of those with the weather the way it's been. And if you should happen to find a barefoot man toasting his friends with his left hand—that will be your man!"

Captain Magirkik left at once and followed my great-great-grandfather's instructions to the letter. He and his deputy immediately began to question Orsha's cobblers, and in the second shop they entered, they found a shoe that exactly matched the bloody print on the floor of the unfortunate grocer's store. The cobbler said he'd never seen the man before and didn't know his name. But he described him as large, bearded, and seemingly very poor.

They took the shoe as evidence, and had barely left the cobbler's shop when another deputy came running to tell them that he had found a barefoot man in rags stumbling aimlessly through the streets. They followed the ragged man until, to their surprise, he turned in at one of Orsha's ritzier pubs, the Brazen Head, where he was greeted warmly by everyone present—though not by name, the captain noticed. The captain and his men took a seat near the door and watched as the poor, barefoot man effusively ordered drinks for the house, and when he raised his glass in his left hand for a toast, they made their move. Two of them held the poor man while the captain himself slipped the shoe onto the man's right foot; and just as he expected, the shoe fit perfectly. They arrested the man and took him to prison to await his trial.

The following week, a front-page article in the Orsha *News* reported that the man who had murdered the grocer had been arrested, tried, and sentenced to ten years at hard labor in the mines of Siberia. The story told all about the vodka, the bloody footprint, and Captain Magirkik's discovery of the culprit in the Brazen Head pub. No mention was made, however, of my great-great-grandfather's role in solving the mystery of the poor barefoot left-handed vodka-drinking murderer. But none was needed. Long before the ink ever dried on the page, the story of Rabbi Shmul's uncanny prescience was the talk of the town, adding further to the legendary reputation of men of the cloth in the time of the czars.

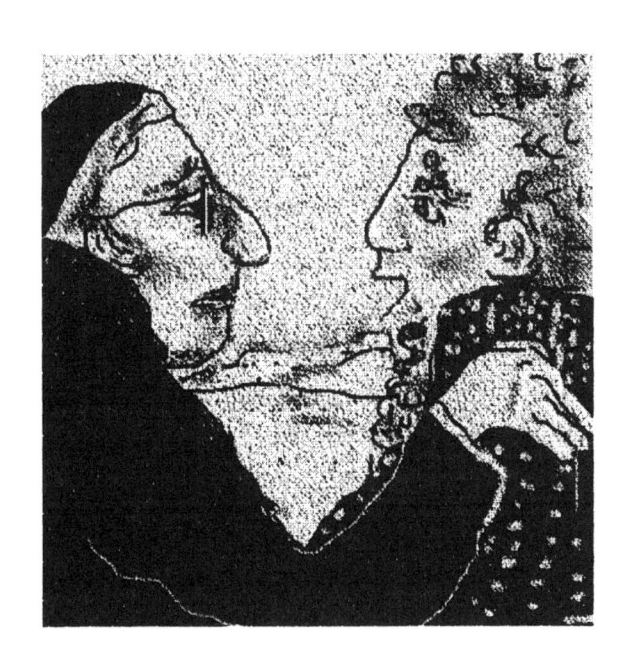

The Stranger

It was about three o'clock on a sunny afternoon when Reb Hashan met a poorly dressed stranger walking through the ghetto. The man looked like he needed help, and he asked Reb Hashan in Yiddish where the rabbi might be found.

Reb Hashan looked the man over before replying. He wore boots that had seen much hard wear, a rumpled and stained pair of trousers that might once have been blue but were now dark gray, a long coat that had seen better days, and a shtreimel trimmed with mangy fur and bleached by the sun to an indefinite hue. His beard, which reached almost to the rope that was tied around his baggy trousers, was tangled and stained with the same streaks that garnished the lapels of his sad coat.

But withal the man had the appearance of vigor. He was large and robust, his broad shoulders filling out his topcoat to its bursted seams. His uncombed hair, brown with streaks of gray, fell over his forehead but did not completely hide his dark eyes, from which an intense light shone, and his ruddy face spoke of the years of hard work that must have been his life. For some reason that Reb Hashan couldn't explain, he felt afraid of the stranger. But the man's perfect command of Yiddish—albeit with a strange accent—assured him that he was a Jew and could mean no harm to the rabbi, and so Reb Hashan directed him to the home of my great-great-grandfather.

As was his custom, Rabbi Shmul was spending the afternoon studying. He had been adding up the numerical values of the words of the prophets, and probing so deeply into their spiritual arcana that he had slipped into a state of reverie bordering on sound sleep, when he was aroused by a knock at the door. That in itself was unusual; nobody in the ghetto ever knocked, they just came right in. But his curiosity was even further piqued when he opened the door to this strange man, who looked more than a little bit like what Grandpa had always imagined the wandering prophet Elijah might look like.

"Come in, please," Grandpa said. "I am Rabbi Shmul ben Shlomo. How may I help you?"

"Thank you, Rabbi," said the man, bowing as he entered. "I am Mika ben Yoshik, and I have just come from Sevastapol. Rabbi, I may be in bad trouble, and I need your advice and perhaps your help. I'm sorry to take your time, but...."

"Not at all," said Rabbi Shmul. "Please sit down and tell me what the matter is."

Grandpa and the stranger sat at the table, and the rebbitsin, Helga, brought out her famous tea and mandelbrot, which the stranger gobbled greedily before continuing.

"Thank you, Rebbitsin," he said, brushing the crumbs from his beard into his hand and eating them too. "It is the first thing I've had to eat today, and I've come quite a long way. And I'm afraid I shall not be able to return to my home—though I swear to you, Rabbi, it is not my fault.

"To begin with, let me tell you about myself. I am a fisherman—that is, I was until a few days ago. And though I know I don't look that way, I'm a frummer, just like any other Jew. Well, I have to admit that I've been a little lax in my duties lately. In my younger days I was very faithful that way—attending shul and wearing tefillin almost every day, observing the Sabbath every week, keeping kosher, and so on. But after my parents died several years ago and my dear wife and daughter were killed by those cursed Cossacks—well, Rabbi, I'm ashamed to admit it, but I must tell you the whole truth—I saw no use in those things, and I gave them up.

"Instead I began to spend my days hauling nets through the sea for fish, and my evenings in one of the bars near the harbor, where I'd sit up late and chew the fat with the other fishermen. It wasn't a pretty life, of course, but it was regular and it kept bread on my table. And those fishermen in the bar became a sort of second family to me. We looked out for each other, Jew and gentile alike in the brotherhood of our occupation, and it kept me out of trouble. That is, until a few days ago.

"You see, it was last Monday night—it must have been around ten or eleven—that a fisherman we had never seen before came into the bar. He looked like a rough one, and the way he staggered in let us know that this wasn't the first public house he'd visited that evening. He gave me a very mean look as he came in and went to the bar, and every so often he'd turn around and give me the same look, until I began to feel very uneasy and was about to leave. Then, to my horror, the man heaved himself up from the bar and came straight over to me. I looked the other way, hoping he'd keep going; but then, without warning, he cuffed me a good blow to the ear and sent my shtreimel flying. 'You, Jew boy,' he shouted loud enough for everyone to hear, 'don't you have the manners to take your hat off in a public house?'

"Everything stopped, and I could feel every eye in the place staring at me. I said nothing, but bent to pick up my hat, and all of a sudden he grabbed me by the back of my coat and lifted me clean out of my chair and spun me around until we were face to face. 'This is a Russian bar!' he yelled. 'We don't like Jews drinking our vodka and taking up space in our bar. Now get out, you damned Jew, and don't show your face in here again!' And with that he pushed me toward the door.

"Well, I wasn't going to take it. I was a regular at that bar, and he was the intruder. Who was he to tell me where I could drink? And I wasn't afraid of him, either. I'm not a scrapper, Rabbi, but I've been in my share of tussles, and I know how to take care of myself. I wasn't about to let some vodka-soaked bully push me around. But I didn't do anything. I just stood there waiting until he came after me again, saying, 'What's the matter, Jew? Are you deaf?' He kept yelling like that, but I just stood there until finally he pulled out a knife and lunged at me.

"That was when I knew I had to defend myself. I grabbed his knife hand with my two hands and wrenched the knife away from him and threw it as far away as I could. Then he pounced on me and started beating me with his fists. He was so drunk he couldn't aim, and most of his punches either hit me on the shoulders, where they did no harm, or missed me entirely. But I knew that sooner or later he'd find his mark, if only by accident. So I took my turn at him and landed him a good one, square on the shnozze. Rabbi, I'm not a violent man, but I'm a big man, and sometimes I don't know my own strength. I must have used a little too much force, because that one punch laid him out on the floor flat as a flounder. It looked for all the world like he was dead.

"It was all over in a matter of seconds, and then my friends were around me congratulating me on my victory. But even if the fight was finished, my trouble had only just begun. Because I knew as well as I know my dear mother's name that if the authorities came they'd blame the whole thing on me and haul me off to jail—and I don't need to tell you what my chances would have been then. My friends agreed I must leave immediately—not just the bar, I must leave Sevastapol—and they all chipped in whatever cash they could to help me get away. They're true men, those fishermen, don't let anybody ever tell you different, Rabbi. In all we collected about fifty rubles, and I went straight to the train station and took the first train, which happened to be going north. I got off at Smolensk, but seeing that it was a busy place and wanting to hide myself so the authorities would never find me, I took the next train out, which happened to be the milk run to Orsha. And so here I am."

The stranger heaved a sigh. "Now what can I do, Rabbi? I can't go back to Sevastapol, that's for sure; I'd be arrested before I could say 'L'chayim.' I don't dare go to any other fishing town either, because sooner or later they'd find me there, too, and now I don't know how I'll earn my livelihood. So here I am, deprived of my friends, my home, and my occupation—through no fault of my own, I swear!"

My great-great-grandfather thought for several moments about what he might tell this troubled man. Though dirty and unkempt, the man seemed honest enough, and Grandpa believed that the fight had not been his fault. But he shuddered to think that his visitor had really killed a man. And the stranger was certainly right about one other thing: the police were notoriously ruthless, especially to Jews. They'd never believe he had acted in self-defense, no matter what the man and all his fishermen friends might say. They would believe what they decided to believe, and they'd never believe a Jew was innocent of the murder of a gentile. And if they got their hands on him...well, better not even think about that!

But it seemed unlikely that they would trace him to Orsha, and even if they did, the rabbi was on good terms with the local authorities and might yet be able to help. And so he offered the stranger this advice.

"My friend," he said, "it is a serious affair. If what you say is true, a man has died by your hand, and you must atone for it. But if, as you say, you acted only in self-defense, you may be forgiven. You are welcome to remain here in our ghetto, though of course there's not much fishing to be done around here. On the other hand, there is a large mill here, the Russian Wool Works, and they can always use the help of a strong man. It wouldn't be what you're used to, but you could earn your keep. As for housing, there is a married couple, Reb Shimmek and his wife, Lila-Fink, who are childless and have an extra room to rent; Lila-Fink might even provide your meals, if you like."

For the first time that day, Mika ben Yoshik, the fisherman, smiled. "Thank you, Rabbi. It is more than I could have asked." And over the next few days, everything worked out just as Rabbi Shmul predicted. Reb Shimmek and his wife welcomed their new boarder, and Baron Gayveski gladly accepted the broad-shouldered man at the Wool Works. But most importantly, no police came sniffing around after a missing fisherman.

And so the stranger remained in Orsha the rest of his life, and was a stranger no more. He never spoke to anyone else about his former life as a fisherman, and of course Rabbi Shmul kept his secret. But every so often one of the ghettoites would see him standing on the banks of the Oloscev stream, staring into its running water, watching as it flowed through the ghetto, through Orsha, and out to sea.

The Hat in the Horse Trough

Though the Jews who lived in the ghettos of Russia in the time of the czars were certainly poor, they were not immune to the common human urge to acquire and accumulate things, the same as anyone anywhere anytime. Many families collected chachkas of one kind or another that were handed down from generation to generation; many collected the few foreign stamps or coins that occasionally found their way into the ghetto; some just collected unusual rocks. But for a very few people, the insatiable urge to accumulate things became an obsession, a fetish even, one that could never be satisfied no matter how large their collections grew.

One such person was Solomon Geversky, whom everyone called Reb Sol, and who lived in the ghetto of Sorelsky, not far from Orsha. Reb Sol collected hats. Tall hats, short hats, felt hats and cloth hats; black hats, white hats, gray hats, and brown hats; hats with broad brims, hats with no brims at all—any kind of hat whatsoever, Reb Sol loved and had to have.

Reb Sol began collecting hats when he was fifteen or so, and throughout his adult life he added to his collection four times each year: at Pesach, in the spring; on his birthday, in the summer; after Rosh Hoshannah in the fall; and on his wedding anniversary, in the winter. Of course, he quickly accumulated more hats than he could ever possibly wear, and most of his collection remained on a shelf in a dark closet that was devoted exclusively to his prizes. But that didn't matter. What mattered was that when Reb Sol saw a hat he liked, he had to have it.

Reb Sol lived a very long life, and accumulated an incredible number of hats. When he died no one was quite sure how old he was; but after the funeral, when they counted his hats and divided by four, Methuselah blushed.

The Hat in the Horse Trough

On the fiftieth anniversary of his marriage, Reb Sol decided to splurge on an extra-special hat to commemorate the occasion. It must be a very deluxe hat, he decided, not only because it was his fiftieth anniversary, but also and especially because his dear wife had died the previous spring, and he wanted to honor her memory and their long years together by pulling out all the stops, in his own special way.

So that morning Reb Sol rode the train to Smolensk, the nearest large city, where he spent the entire day browsing the shops of the city's dozen or so hatters. He saw all types of hats—bowlers and stovepipes and fedoras, and even a red fez from Morocco. But although he found them all beautiful, nothing he saw seemed good enough for this special occasion.

Finally, just before dusk, he found it. In a small, dark shop along a back alley near the market district, perched on a stand behind a grimy window, was a beautiful high-crowned brown beaver hat with a broad black ribbon. Reb Sol froze in his tracks, and he stood in aesthetic arrest. Even through the sooty window, he could see the lustrous sheen of the hat's crown and the fine, even lay of the rich brown beaver fur. Trembling a little (partly because he hadn't eaten all day), he entered the shop and asked if he might try on the hat. It fit perfectly! He looked at himself in the mirror that sat on the counter, and saw the reflection of a czar, a king, a pasha.

Reb Sol didn't even take the hat off, but bought it on the spot. It took every kopek he had, but it was worth it, well worth it—a bargain at twice the price, and Reb Sol left the shop as proud as he ever could be.

On the train home, Reb Sol finally took off the hat, out of deference to his fellow passengers and also because he was afraid the high crown would bump up against the handrails on the ceiling and become soiled or dented. He sat silent as a stone during the entire trip, contemplating the hat in his lap like Buddha lost in meditation, a faint smile playing at the corners of his mouth. By the time the train reached Orsha, he had decided that this would be his special Shabbes hat, to be worn only to the shul once a week, every week, on top of his yarmulka. Never mind that another fifty-one hats in his collection would go unworn as a result. A Shabbes hat was a Shabbes hat, and this was it. When he got home he carefully wrapped the new beaver hat in tissue and put it on the highest shelf in the hat closet, there to await the Shabbes.

Came the Shabbes, and the weather turned nasty. Snow was falling hard and fast, and a stiff wind blew out of the north. As Reb Sol dressed for shul, he looked out the window and then at his new hat. Should he really risk the hat on such a blizzard? But then, he thought, the hat was made of beaver, and a little snow and wind never bothered any beaver, had it? So why not? He put on his overcoat and shawl, and pulled his new hat down firmly to his ears, then set out for shul.

Reb Sol hadn't gone twenty steps before he was hit by a blast of wind that had apparently left the north pole in a big a hurry to get to Odessa. The wind tugged at his coat, pulled on his shawl, then whipped about his ears and snatched the new beaver hat right off Reb Sol's head. As Reb Sol watched helplessly, the hat sailed through the air for several meters, turning graceful cartwheels among the falling snowflakes, then rolled on its brim through the snow like a champion figure skater and fetched up against a fresh heap of dung.

When Reb Sol picked up the hat, his heart sank. There was a huge dark glob stuck to its lustrous crown. He cleaned it off as best he could, and holding the hat firmly to his head he continued on to the shul, where, to his delight, it elicited all the ooohs and ahhhs it truly deserved.

The next morning Reb Sol gave the hat to Natishka, the cleaning lady who had been coming to help him twice a week ever since his wife died. Natishka was a diligent woman, though perhaps not the brightest person Reb Sol had ever met, and it was with some reservation that he gave her his favorite hat.

"This is my very best hat," he explained carefully. "It's my Shabbes hat. So be very careful with it."

"Don't you worry," Natishka chirped, hardly listening to Reb Sol's admonishment. "I'll clean it good as new, just you wait and see."

That very evening, Natishka got out her boar-bristle brush and a fresh cake of lye soap and set to work on Reb Sol's hat. The dung stain had dried hard and had more or less set into the thick beaver fur, and it took quite a bit of rubbing and scrubbing and almost half the cake of lye soap before it all came out.

Unfortunately, however, the stain was not all that came out. As she rinsed the hat, Natishka was horrified to see that large patches of the fine beaver fur had also fallen out, and as she tried to brush what remained to cover up the bald spot, more and more of the rich dark fur fell into her lap.

But the ever-resourceful Natishka was not alarmed. Beaver, shmeaver, she thought; brown fur is brown fur. She had an old coat of rabbit skin that she hardly ever wore, anyway, of a color that matched Reb Sol's beaver hat exactly, almost. It took her only a few minutes to cut a few pieces from the old coat and patch them into the hat, and when it was finished, if you didn't look too carefully you couldn't even tell the difference, hardly. As the coup de grace, and as a special favor to Reb Sol, of whom she was very fond, she took a length of red ribbon that she had been saving and carefully sewed it around the base of the hat's crown, where it looked quite festive, she thought.

She scrunched up her eyes and admired her work. If you held it just right under the dim light of the oil lamp, you couldn't even see where it had been mended, very much. It looked as good as new, practically—better, even, with the ribbon.

The next morning Natishka set out to deliver her handiwork to Reb Sol. She had the hat carefully wrapped, and she clutched it tightly to her breast as she gingerly navigated the wintry streets, which had become quite icy overnight. She was almost to her employer's home when along came a Russian peasant on a huge farm wagon overloaded with broken limbs of trees that had been downed by the blizzard. She didn't even see it coming, but one of the projecting limbs caught her in the back and sent her flying. The hat, too, went flying, and with the help of an errant breeze sailed directly into a nearby horse trough full of water.

Natishka picked herself up and brushed off the snow. Fortunately she was not hurt—a little bruised, perhaps, but entire. Sadly, however, the same could not be said for Reb Sol's hat. It was completely soaked, and one of the rabbit fur patches was starting to come loose. One look was all that Natishka needed to see that this time the hat was ruined beyond repair.

What should she do? Reb Sol would be furious if he saw the hat like this. Of course, it wasn't her fault, she knew that. But would Reb Sol understand? She'd only known him a few months, and she didn't know him well enough to be sure. One thing she did know, however, was that in his old age Reb Sol had become extremely forgetful. So, as she weighed her options, she realized that there was a good chance that if she did nothing and said nothing, Reb Sol might never ask about it. She looked around at the empty streets and, satisfied that no one had witnessed the accident, went on her way and left the hat in the horse trough.

As it turned out, Natishka was right. The next Friday when she arrived to help clean Reb Sol's house, he made no mention of the high-crowned beaver hat. After a little while she began to relax, but she froze in her tracks when Reb Sol, dressed and ready to go to the shul, asked, "Natishka, have you seen my new Shabbes hat?"

Natishka gulped. "Why…er…no…Reb Sol, I haven't seen it in days," she said, which was true. Together they riffled through the hat closet and searched all three rooms of the tiny house, but of course they didn't find the hat. Finally, when the hour grew late and the hat was still not found, Reb Sol said, "Well, I suppose I'll have to wear another one instead. This black one will do. But I

The Hat in the Horse Trough

can't imagine where I've put my Shabbes hat. If I keep losing things like this, I'll lose my own head one of these days. Old age, Natishka, old age—it's terrible, terrible!" Thus muttering, Reb Sol tottered off to the shul wearing his black felt hat.

It was nighttime by the time the service ended, but the moon was extraordinarily bright in the clear winter sky, and its reflection in the snow made it nearly bright as day. Thus it was that as Reb Sol was passing by a horse trough near his home, he noticed something sticking up from the thin skin of ice that had formed on the surface of the water.

Curious, he stopped to investigate, and to his surprise and delight, what should he find but a hat! He punched away the ice and pulled out the hat, which was frozen just about stiff and looked shiny as a blue sapphire in the moonlight. It was a high-crowned hat, he observed, constructed of a variety of different furs that gave it an unusual variegated texture, and around the brim was a strip of bright red ribbon that made it look quite festive, he thought. Gingerly, for the hat was cold and wet, he held it to his head. It fit perfectly!

What an unexpected boon, he thought—a new hat for an old man! Reb Sol never for a moment recognized that the ragged, frozen hat was his own.

Reb Sol put his new prize under his arm and carried it home, where he dried it carefully by the fire and tucked it away on the top shelf of the hat closet, where it remained. He never wore it, not even once. And he never did figure out where he'd put his Shabbes beaver hat.

The Rabbi's Shabbes Shoes

Yusky Havalsky, a handyman in the ghetto of Orsha in the time of the czars, was a kind of Jack of all trades. He had no particular specialty (nor, to tell the whole truth, any particular talent), but he performed all kinds of work adequately enough, and when someone needed plumbing repaired, a shed built, or a roof mended, they usually went to Reb Yusky.

Reb Yusky's dearest friend was Denisco, whom everybody called Den, and who owned a grocery store called "The Best of the Best" in the ghetto of

Smolensk. If ever Den needed work done on his store, he would send a message to Yusky in Orsha, and Yusky would come running to help his friend.

One spring day Yusky received such a message, and he dropped what he was doing (he had been helping to raise the fence between the yards of two neighbors so that one particular rooster wouldn't keep jumping over it) and prepared to leave on the next train for Smolensk. As he was dressing, however, he discovered that there was a tiny hole in the sole of one of his good shoes (the right one).

Now, Yusky was no Beau Brummel, but he was careful about his appearance. Under no circumstances would it do to arrive in Smolensk with a hole in his shoe. There was no question of getting the shoe fixed on such short notice. And there was no way he would wear his everyday shoes, stained and worn as they were, on a trip to the city. Yusky was at a loss; what should he do? Where could he turn for help?

Of course, the one place all ghettoites turned to for help was the home of my great-great-grandfather, Rabbi Shmul ben Shlomo, and that's exactly where Yusky headed, wearing his workaday shoes and carrying his good ones. Over a cup of tea and the requisite slice of Rebbitsin Helga's famous mandelbrot, Yusky laid his woes before the rabbi.

"Rabbi, my dear friend Den—you know him, from Smolensk?—his store was terribly damaged in the storm on Saturday. He thinks it was hit by lightning, and now there's a big hole in the roof and water everywhere. I've got to go help him, Rabbi. But look..." He held out his right dress shoe, and the light shone through the hole in the sole. "I can't go like this to Smolensk. What would people think, that I'm some kind of shnorrer?"

Rabbi Shmul hid his smile under his heavy moustache, which he always left untrimmed for precisely this purpose. After a moment in which he seemed to reflect on this weighty matter—but in which he actually worked to suppress a chuckle, he said, "Well, perhaps you could borrow my shoes, if they're not too small. They're the shoes I wear to the shul for Shabbes service, and since today is only Monday, I suppose I can let them go for a few days, if you'll promise to take care of them."

Reb Yusky was overjoyed. He never would have asked to borrow the rabbi's shoes, although in truth, he had come hoping the rabbi would offer them. But his eyes really popped when he saw the shoes. They looked like new—in fact, they practically *were* new. Rabbi Shmul wore them only on his way to and from the shul on the Shabbes; when he arrived, he would take them off and change into a pair of soft, rubber-soled cloth shoes. He preferred to wear the cloth shoes during prayers for three reasons: for one, leather shoes were a sign of wealth, which was not appropriate for a prayer service, especially during the high holy days; for another, a shoe of leather meant that some animal had been killed to supply the materials, and that wasn't appropriate either; the third reason—and the real clincher—was that the leather shoes pinched the rabbi's toes, taking his mind off his devotions and setting it on his corns.

And so, with many thanks and a promise to take meticulous care of them, Reb Yusky accepted the rabbi's shoes, laced them on tightly, and made straightaway for the station, where he boarded a third-class coach for Smolensk.

Arrived in Smolensk, Yusky went directly to the shop of his friend Den, where he found everything in disarray. There was a black-fringed hole in the roof as big as a cow, and puddles of rainwater and piles of sodden merchandise lay everywhere. Denisco was in a state. "Vey is mir!" he exclaimed as he toured his friend among the flayed cabbages, squashed tomatoes, and sacks of flour that had already begun to form a pasty mess. "What are we going to do about all this mess?"

"Don't you worry, Deni," said Yusky, stepping gingerly to keep the rabbi's shoes clean. "We'll have this fixed up in no time. You have a ladder, don't you? Let me take a closer look at that roof."

Denisco set up the ladder, and Yusky climbed

to the top. The roof looked bad, but not beyond repair. The bird's-eye view of the mess below was horrible, but all that was really wrong was a couple of overturned shelves. A lot of merchandise was ruined, but no fixtures had actually been broken.

"It doesn't look so bad, really," Yusky called down to his friend as he started to climb back down the ladder.

Then, suddenly, a little gust of wind puffed up. Not much of a wind, just a breath; but enough to loosen a shingle from the edge of the hole in the roof and cause it to fall down right on Yusky's head. With a shout, Yusky fell down the ladder all the way to the floor.

"Yusky!" cried Denisco. "Are you all right?"

Fortunately, Yusky had landed in a heap of cabbages, which had broken his fall. He wasn't hurt, but as he plucked bits of cabbage from his clothes, he looked down and to his horror noticed that although he was all right, the rabbi's dress shoes were not! His right foot had scraped against the rungs of the ladder on his way down, and there was a huge scuff mark right across the toebox of the rabbi's right shoe.

"Oy, vey is *mir*," it was now his turn to wail. "These are Rabbi Shmul's best shoes, and now they're ruined! What can I do?" For once, there was absolutely nowhere for him to turn.

"Not to worry, not to worry," Denisco consoled

him. He went behind the counter and reached up on a shelf and took down a bottle of shoe polish. "This ought to fix it right up."

But the polish did little. It was nothing but a cheap solution of charcoal and alcohol, and the dull, streaky finish it left when it had dried only made the scuffmark look worse.

Still Denisco was confident. "Not to worry, not to worry. My brother-in-law is a cobbler, and his shop is only a few blocks away. We'll go right now; I'm sure he can fix the shoe."

Together they went around to the cobbler's shop, where they found Denisco's brother-in-law at work on an old boot.

"Hmm," he said, peering over his spectacles as Yusky and Den watched anxiously. "Hmm, hmm, hmm," he said again, shaking his head. "You say you fell off a ladder, did you? In Deni's shop? And what is this all over the scuff? Shoe polish, you say? Hmm…" and he set the shoe down on the counter, where it looked as forlorn as a scuffed shoe—which, of course, it was. "All I can offer to do is polish it up real good. But it won't look like new. It will never look like new, because it will never be new. How can you expect me to make it look new, nu?"

"Please," said Yusky, "it's our rabbi's shoe, and I promised to take care of it. Can't you try?"

"Well," said the cobbler, "if you'll leave it here, I'll do what I can. But it won't look like new again. I'm sorry, but that's the way it is."

Yusky left the shoe, and he and Den returned to the grocery store. Den loaned him a pair of work boots, and they spent the rest of that day and most of the next working on the hole in the roof of the store, with the help of several boys from the ghetto. By the end of the second day the store looked as good as new, almost, and Yusky returned to the cobbler to pick up the rabbi's shoe.

"Well," said the cobbler, "I did what I could. It doesn't look new, but...."

Yusky held the shoe to the light. It was shiny as could be, and if the light was at the right angle, you could hardly see the scuff. But the cobbler had been right; it simply wasn't a new shoe anymore. He'd have to apologize to Rabbi Shul; that was all he could do. That evening, with a heavy heart in his breast, the rabbi's shoes in his hand, and a pair of Denisco's boots on his feet, he took the third-class train back to Orsha.

To Yusky's relief, Rabbi Shmul seemed not to be bothered at all by the scuff mark on his Shabbes shoe. "Accidents happen," he said. "And it doesn't matter so much, anyway. I only wear them for looks, and what are looks? Just looks! I appreciate your honesty, though, and I appreciate your having it polished so nicely. Don't worry, Yusky, I don't think anyone will ever notice the difference." With those soothing remarks in his ear, Yusky returned to his home and felt much better about the whole thing.

But Rabbi Shmul was wrong for once. People did notice, and it did make a difference, though not in any way he might have imagined. The very next Shabbes he wore his dress shoes to the shul, but because he was a little late he didn't have time to change into his comfy cloth shoes before the service, and so he was still wearing the shoes as he stood on the bima reciting the prayers.

Also seated on the bima was the president of the shul, Reb Khasel Honsky. It was Reb Khasel's duty as president to make announcements to the congregation of such news as illnesses, deaths, special events in the community, or special needs of the shul. Most often, however, he just sat there and recited prayers like everyone else. On this particular evening, as Khasel Honsky sat waiting for his turn to speak, he noticed that one of the rabbi's shoes was badly scuffed.

Oy, he though to himself as the prayers droned on, just look at those shoes. Scuffed! And see how he's tried to hide it with polish. Such a shande that our rabbi has to wear old worn-out shoes! What would people think? Maybe we don't pay him enough. A rabbi ought to be able to afford a decent pair of shoes, after all. I'll have to ask the shul board to give him a raise. Scuffed shoes should never be worn by our rabbi—especially on the Shabbes!

And so, at the next meeting of the shul's board of directors, Khasel Honsky broke the news that their esteemed and beloved Rabbi Shmul was so underpaid that he was forced to wear worn-out shoes to Shabbes service. "It's a public embarrassment," he insisted, "and I think we ought to give Rabbi Shmul a raise of five rubles a month. I also suggest that we not embarrass him by saying anything about the shoes. Let's just give him the raise and tell him how proud we are that he is our rabbi." The board agreed and the resolution was adopted, and Khasel Honsky himself went to give Rabbi Shmul the good news.

And so it was in this strange and complicated way that Rabbi Shmul received the one and only raise in salary he ever got while serving as head of the Orsha congregation. Just think of the incredible chain of events and coincidents that occurred, each of which was indispensable in getting Grandpa the raise: first, the lightning that struck the store of Yusky's friend Den; second, Yusky's trip to Smolensk to help his friend; third, the hole in the sole of one of Yusky's shoes; fourth, my great-great-grandfather's generosity in lending his own shoes to Yusky; fifth, the scuffing of the rabbi's right shoe when Yusky fell off the ladder; sixth, the rabbi's tardiness that day, which caused him to wear the scuffed leather shoes instead of the cloth shoes during the service; and seventh, Khasel Honsky's observation of the rabbi's scuffed shoe. What are the chances?

It is true, as they say, that God—blessed be His holy name—works in strange and mysterious ways. Very strange and mysterious, indeed!

Not Guilty

Reb Haskel ben Robishka was a cabinetmaker who lived in the ghetto of Orsha, and probably one of the most talented cabinetmakers who ever lived anywhere. His furniture was simply beautiful—the richly grained wood flawlessly matched, the dovetail joints nearly invisible, and the corners so perfectly square that the doors to his cabinets opened and closed as quietly as a cloud floating through a blue sky.

Reb Haskel's skill was well known, not only in the ghetto and the rest of Orsha, but throughout the Byelorussian countryside. Orders came from as far away as Smolensk, and even beyond. There was always more work available than Reb Haskel could ever accept, and so he had the luxury of accepting only those jobs which offered him the best opportunity to practice his craft, and he always charged what his work was worth, never scrimping on materials or on the hand-carved details that made his furniture so unique.

Of course, Reb Haskel was not the only cabinetmaker in Orsha. In the Russian section of town lived another, one Manski Shmudik, a man who was in every way Reb Haskel's polar opposite. Reb Haskel was an upstanding, clean-living member of the community, but Manski Shmudik was a notorious drunkard and wife-beater. And whereas Reb Haskel's work was fine and meticulous and took weeks to complete, Manski Shmudik's was careless and slapdash, usually thrown together in the few hours between the time the old sod lolled out of bed and the time the pubs opened in the afternoon. Reb Haskel built his armoires, tables, and sideboards so that they would last a lifetime, while Manski Shmudik only made sure that a few well-placed gobs of glue held his heaps together long enough for him to get his clients' money into a glass and down his gullet. On the other hand, whereas Reb Haskel's fine furniture was rather expensive, Manski Shmudik's was dirt cheap; and since economics often dictate to taste, there was quite a bit more of Manski Shmudik's shlock than of Reb Haskel's artwork to be found in the homes of Orsha.

One day there came a commission from Baron Gayveski, the wealthy owner of the Russian Wool Works and one of the political bosses of the area. For months the baron had endured his wife's complaints that their home needed new cabinetry in the kitchen, new shelves in the library, and a new set of table and chairs in the parlor; now he had finally relented and agreed to call in a couple of woodworkers for bids.

The two he called were Reb Haskel and Manski Shmudik, and at different times the same day, each of them visited the baron's home to learn about the job, inspect the house, and offer his bid.

The first to arrive was Reb Haskel, the first Jew other than Rabbi Shmul ever to set foot inside the mansion. As the baron's wife escorted him through the rooms and described what she wanted done, Reb Haskel was overwhelmed by the opulence of the place. There were chandeliers in every room, oaken doors so heavy (and so poorly hung, he noted) that you had to lean on them to make them budge, and window casings that belonged in a cathedral, not in someone's home. What a privilege it would be to build cabinetry for such a splendid house, he thought. He quickly sketched plans that would complement the gracious home, and wrote out a bid that he knew would fit the baron's pocketbook.

Manski Shmudik, on the other hand, arrived late for his appointment, having just come from quaffing the winnings of a bet he had placed on a dog race that afternoon. He belched at the chandeliers, ran his dirty fingers over the casement windows, and farted loudly as he pushed open the heavy oaken doors. After just a few minutes of careless inspection, he submitted a bid that, he calculated, would just about cover a week-long spree at his favorite pub, a seedy place called the Green Pig.

That evening the baron and his wife compared the two bids. The baron, a penny-pincher with no great love for Jews, was immediately in favor of Manski Shmudik's bid, which looked like a bargain to him. But his wife, who had been more than a little put off by Shmudik's behavior, argued in favor of Reb Haskel, whose work would certainly be superior. In the end it was of course she who prevailed, and the next morning both workmen were advised that the contract would be awarded to Reb Haskel.

When Manski Shmudik got the news he was furious. "What right has that damn Jew to take work from an honest Russian?" he demanded of his wife, who was the nearest person upon whom he could vent his rage. "You can't trust those Jews to compete fairly like honest men. That silver-tongued devil probably filled the baroness full of lies to get on her good side—and once he got on the good side, he probably filled her full of something else, too, I don't doubt!" On and on he raved, spouting the same kind of nonsense, until he finally drove his poor wife to tears. Having exhausted his limited supply of words, he went on to vent himself with his fists, beating his wife severely. Then he summoned his carriage driver and rode to his favorite pub to plan his revenge.

No one greeted Manski Shmudik as he pushed his way into the pub grumbling. They never did, unless he had just been paid for a job and was in a mood to buy drinks for the house. But this time he sank down at a dark corner table, and after the bartender had brought him his usual beer and schnapps, he sat there unblinking, his mind churning like a plow through mud, until finally a dim light went on inside him and he slowly got up and made his way out of the pub. "Let's go," he snapped at his driver. "We've got a score to settle at Reb Haskel's, you and I."

Reb Haskel was surprised to see Manski Shmudik at his door. His arch-rival had never come to see him before (nor had Reb Haskel ever hoped he would). And Reb Haskel was also a little alarmed; for Shmudik's breath reeked of schnapps, and the way his eyes slunk back and forth in his head told Reb Haskel that whatever Shmudik was up to, it was surely no good.

"Afternoon, good sir," slurred Shmudik unctuously. "Congratulations on the Gayveski job. I've got a little tip that might help you with it; may I come inside?"

No gentile had ever entered Reb Haskel's home before, but despite his suspicions Reb Haskel wanted to be polite, so he opened the door wide and Manski Shmudik stumbled in. Just as Reb Haskel was closing the door, Shmudik caught hold of his arm and, looking sneakily around him said, "It's cold outside; may my driver come in also?" Again Reb Haskel felt he could not refuse. "But of course," he said, and Shmudik summoned the driver inside with a rude yell.

No sooner had the driver come in and sat down than Manski Shmudik sprang into action. It all happened so fast that Reb Haskel could barely believe it. In one swift motion, Shmudik drew a gleaming dagger from his sleeve and without warning plunged it to the hilt into his driver's chest. The surprised driver's eyes bulged wide, and with a horrifying gurgle the man fell to the floor in a pool of blood. At once Shmudik ran out the front door and into the street, where he stood shouting at the top of his lungs, "Help! Murder! Police! That Jew has killed my driver!"

Before a crowd could assemble, Reb Haskel, seized with panic, ran out the back door, across the fields behind his house, to the home of Rabbi Shmul. Clearly, Manski Shmudik must have been trying to get even with him by framing him for the murder of his driver. He explained it all to

Rabbi Shmul, stumbling through his account and making almost no sense at all, until the rabbi interrupted him with a hand on his arm.

"Reb Haskel, you must hurry now. There is no time to lose," he said, glancing at his watch. "You must do exactly as I say. You must go at once to the station and take the next train to Smolensk—it leaves in five minutes. And you must ride in the first-class car. Do you understand? You must ride first-class." Rabbi Shmul took a small roll of banknotes from his coat pocket and peeled off a few, which he gave to the distraught cabinetmaker. "This will cover your fare; you can't go home for your wallet, and you haven't time. Now go, quickly!"

"But, Rabbi," protested Reb Haskel, "what am I to do in Smolensk?"

But the rabbi didn't answer the question. "Go," he said, "now," and he shoved Reb Haskel out the back door.

Reb Haskel made it to the station just in time to hear the conductor blow his whistle, and he jumped on the train even as it began to move. He stood in the companionway for a moment and composed himself, then made his way down the aisle of a first-class car, looking for a seat. All of the compartments were occupied, most with businessmen on their errands, and Reb Haskel felt conspicuously out of place among them. Like all Jews, he had only ever ridden third-class, and the businessmen's fine suits and tall hats made his own worn clothing look even shabbier than usual. Finally he found a compartment with one vacant seat, but the three men inside were so well dressed that Reb Haskel didn't dare to enter. But then one of the men, either not noticing how Reb Haskel was dressed or not caring, motioned him inside.

"Come in, we've got plenty of room. It's unusually crowded today, isn't it?" said the man pleasantly. Reb Haskel didn't know whether it was unusually crowded or anything else, but he was relieved to find a seat.

"You seem upset, friend," said another of the men. "I hope everything is all right?"

Without thinking, Reb Haskel unburdened himself to the three gentlemen. He never considered that his story might get him into trouble all over again, but told them every detail as clearly as he remembered it. The only thing he omitted was that he was a Jew, for there was no telling how these men, who were obviously gentiles, would react; they would surely assume that he had committed the murder himself. But the three men sat silently listening to the strange story, and when Reb Haskel had finished, they offered neither comment nor advice, but only nodded in sympathy.

By the time Reb Haskel had finished the grisly tale the train was already nearing the Smolensk station, and the three gentlemen rose to leave. Reb Haskel followed them onto the platform, where they bade him goodbye and wished him luck. Then he found himself standing there alone, the crowd of travelers buzzing all around him, without the least idea where he should go or what he should do. Rabbi Shmul had ordered him to Smolensk, and here he was. Now what?

Reb Haskel supposed he must wait in Smolensk until the heat died down, so he passed three days idling in the marketplace and along the riverbank, his mind in a turmoil. What was happening back home in Orsha? Were the police looking for him? If so, they couldn't be looking too hard, or they would have found him by now, even in Smolensk. And what about his house? He had left without even closing the door.

Finally he could stand it no longer. He couldn't stay in Smolensk forever. But what would happen if he tried to go home? Surely Rabbi Shmul had thought of that. Come what may, he had to go home sooner or later, and so on the fourth day he begged a few rubles to buy a third-class ticket, and took the train back home.

When he got to Orsha and stepped off the train, the police were waiting for him. Reb Haskel was arrested and taken to jail for the murder of Manski Shmudik's driver.

For two days Reb Haskel remained alone in a dark cell, wondering what would become of him.

It was the end, he was sure. Few Jews ever saw the inside of a Russian prison and lived to tell about it. What had gone wrong, he wondered? Where was Rabbi Shmul now?

Then, on the third day, a guard came to his cell and told Reb Haskel to get up, he was going to trial. This would be it, he thought to himself. They would read the charges, render the verdict, and have him hung the same day. But when the guard pushed him into the courtroom, he got the surprise of his life. Seated high on the judge's bench was none other than the man who had invited him to share his first-class compartment on the train to Smolensk! And as Reb Haskel looked about the room he was further amazed to see that the prosecutor and the public defender were the other two men to whom he had told his sad story that day. At the back of the room, among the small crowd of the curious, nosy, and just plain idle people who spend their time attending trials, sat Rabbi Shmul. He caught Reb Haskel's eye and gave him a knowing smile.

The judge banged his gavel for silence and asked the bailiff to read the charges against Reb Haskel. Then he asked the prosecutor to call his first witness.

"Your honor," said the prosecutor, "we will call no witnesses."

A buzz arose among the spectators, and Reb Haskel felt his head spinning. Was the case against him so open-and-shut that no witnesses would be required? At least Rabbi Shmul was there, he thought, to come to his defense. But when the defense, too, declined to call a witness, Reb Haskel knew it was all over. He was being railroaded, pure and simple, as so many defendants often were—especially Jews.

But what happened next Reb Haskel could never have imagined. When both attorneys were again seated, the judge leaned over the bench and addressed the court. "Gentlemen," he said, "six days ago Mr. Slonimsky, the prosecutor, Mr. Vrenedy, the public defender, and I were on the train to Smolensk, where we happened to meet Mr. Haskel, who was also on his way to Smolensk. Mr. Haskel did not know who we were, nor did we know who he was, and with complete candor Mr. Haskel told us how he had witnessed the murder of Mr. Gravsky, the driver, by his own master, Mr. Shmudik, in Mr. Haskel's home. Under the circumstances, we were very inclined to believe Mr. Haskel—the more so considering Mr. Haskel's character and reputation against those of his accuser, Mr. Shmudik."

Now the gallery was abuzz with whispers of astonishment. Since when did the court of the czar take the word of a Jew for anything? It was unbelievable—a travesty! But that wasn't yet the end of it. The judge banged his gavel and called for order, and when the crowd quieted, he continued.

"In the meantime, the court has received the affidavit of its own investigator. Two days ago, in the public house known as the Green Pig, Mr. Shmudik was overheard to explain to his companions how he had conspired to both rid himself of his driver, whom he felt to be dishonest and unreliable, and simultaneously to obtain revenge against Mr. Haskel, whom he felt had cheated him out of a contract with Baron Gayveski. His plan was to murder the driver in Mr. Haskel's home and blame Mr. Haskel for the crime. A warrant was then issued for the arrest of Mr. Shmudik, but he has not been found; it seems he has decided to try his luck elsewhere."

Again the crowd gasped as one, and again the judge banged his gavel for order.

"Therefore," he concluded, "in consideration of these facts as presented to us, the court orders that Mr. Haskel be remanded into the custody of his rabbi, Mr. Shmul. This case shall be held in abeyance pending the discovery and arrest of Mr. Shmudik—should that ever occur—at which time it shall proceed until a verdict is rendered. Bailiff, please release the defendant; Mr. Haskel, you are free to go."

There was a great celebration in the ghetto that night for the first Jew ever to come before a Russian court of law and walk away a free man. And although everyone was jubilant, after Reb Haskel himself it was Rabbi Shmul who seemed the most joyful.

"You have surely helped me, Rabbi," said Reb Haskel. "But how did you do it? You must have known that the judge and those lawyers would be on the train; but how did you know?"

"Ah," said Rabbi Shmul, brushing crumbs of mandelbrot from his beard, "because it was Friday." Reb Haskel looked puzzled, so my great-great-grandfather continued, "As everyone knows, there is no court on Fridays. People think it is so that the judges and attorneys can get their paperwork done, but I know different. For when I was a boy and worked as a go-fer for the newspaper, I always made sure to be in Smolensk on Friday afternoon so that I might attend the dog races, which are always held on Friday. And there at the racetrack, all the legal minds from miles around gather in the clubhouse to place their bets and talk shop. I know those three gentlemen well, for I first met them at the racetrack when they were just students and I a lowly go-fer, and I know they'd never miss a Friday afternoon dog race— even if they had to close the courts to do it. I knew they'd be on that train, and I knew you'd run into them. I hoped—no, I prayed—that if they heard of this case from you first, they'd recognize the truth that comes from a man who is afraid for his life. And, thank God—blessed be His holy name—they did."

The Matzo Mitzvah

In the ghetto of Orsha, the approach of Pesach brought on a hurricane of activity. Along with Rosh Hoshanah and Yom Kippur, Pesach was then, as now, one of the most special days of the Jewish calendar. And given the difficulties of ghetto life, the ghettoites devoted themselves to observing the holiday with meticulous care. Everything had to be done exactly the right way, and not a detail must be overlooked—especially when it came to the strict kosher rules for Pesach. And as often happened, the people would sometimes go a little overboard; but even in this, an unexpected mitzvah might sometimes be hidden.

Preparations began weeks before the holiday with a thorough cleansing of every household to remove every trace of chometz, leavened breads and the like, from the premises. Not a crumb must remain if a household was to be considered truly kosher in the sense that Pesach demanded. And so families organized impromptu search parties, with husbands and wives, children and grandparents, one and all emptying the cupboards, turning drawers inside out, crawling under furniture and fixtures to find that last hidden crumb that must surely be lurking in some unlikely place. Not only were the shelves and walls scrubbed down and the closets and pantries swept vigorously, but if, for example, a child should find an old crust of bread in the pocket of his coat, the coat itself would have to be washed so that not an atom of chometz would remain.

The same held true for bakeries where kosher matzo was prepared for Pesach. Instead of bread, during Pesach all the ghettoites of Orsha ate matzo, as Jews have always done and always will do. It is called the "bread of affliction," eaten by the Israelites as they fled Egypt, and to eat those dry, tasteless wafers of flour and water reminds Jews of the tribulations of their ancestors. Of course, it was a big job to provide kosher matzo for every resident of the ghetto, especially under such strict rules of cleanliness. In the larger cities, such as Smolensk, bakeries were shut down for days while they were cleaned from top to bottom under the strict supervision of one of the local rabbis. But in Orsha this was not practical; the ghetto's few bakeries were all housed in such old buildings that there was no hope of removing a whole year's worth of flour dust from the millions of chinks, cracks, and crannies that lined the walls.

Instead, in the Orsha ghetto, each year one woman from a group of related families would take her turn at making matzo for all—sisters and brothers, aunts and uncles, cousins, nieces, and nephews. People who had no family—widows and bachelors, for example—would be "adopted" for Pesach and provided with matzo; or they could "subscribe" to another extended family and take their turns at baking matzo along with the rest. Thus the women whose turn it was would be at it for days, mixing and rolling and baking. Arduous it surely was, but the harder each one worked and the more relatives she provided for, the longer it would be until her turn came around again. And so she would work until her kitchen was so full of fresh, kosher matzo that there simply wasn't room for her to work anymore.

One particular year, the year that became known as the Year of the Matzo Mitzvah, it was Malka-Vana's turn to make matzo for all her family's families. Malka-Vana was the wife of Reb Beno ben Baldo, a farmer who was one of the more affluent (that is to say, least poor) citizens of the ghetto. Theirs was a large family, indeed; for in addition to their own four children, Reb Beno had five siblings, and Malka-Vana had eight. Each of these was married and had his or her own brood of four or five little ones, not to mention in-laws, grandparents, and already a few grandchildren. But Malka-Vana looked forward to her turn at matzo making; this would be her first chance to give her family such a gift, and at the rate the family was growing, it might also be her last.

Unfortunately, just a day or so before Malka-Vana was to begin baking, an accident occurred. She and her husband had taken their horse and small wagon to the fields to gather tomatoes as extra holiday treats for the family, and they had just started home with several bushel baskets of plump red fruits when, without warning, one of the wheels came loose from its axle. Reb Beno, who was walking alongside, managed to jump out of the way; but there was nothing he could do to stop the heavy wagon from toppling. Malka-Vana, who was riding in the wagon, was thrown into the road amid a hail of tomatoes such as the worst vaudevillian never saw, and when Reb Beno reached her she was clutching her leg and moaning in pain.

As quickly as he could, Reb Beno reattached the wheel to the wagon and brought his wife to

Dr. Shatsky, who at once diagnosed a broken femur. With some difficulty he set it and held the bones in place with plaster bandages, then gave Malka-Vana a small dose of tincture of opium for the pain and admonished her to stay off her feet for at least two weeks.

Even greater than the pain of her broken leg was Malka-Vana's disappointment: there was no way she would be able to bake matzo as she had planned, and she had so looked forward to it! Fortunately, though, with such a big family there was never any doubt that she and Reb Beno would have all the matzo they needed, for every woman in the family was ready to leap into the breach.

That same evening Malka-Vana's sister Shura came to visit. "Poor thing!" she exclaimed, "and just before the holiday. But don't worry, I'll bake the matzo this year, and you can take my turn next year."

"Thank you, sister," said Malka-Vana, more grateful to have her turn at baking rescheduled than to be relieved of her duty.

Not an hour later, Malka-Vana's Aunt Taufel arrived at her bedside. "Not to worry about a thing," she soothed. "I'll make the matzo this year."

"Thank you, Auntie," said Malka-Vana, "but Sister Shura has said...."

"Shush, girl, no argument. You must rest!" And

with that Aunt Taufel left. Now there were two women who had promised to bake matzo for her, but Malka-Vana didn't worry about it. She took her aunt's advice and fell asleep.

The next morning her cousin Rachel came, followed by another sister, Leika, followed by a niece, Vankya. They each promised to make matzo for Malka-Vana and her family, and when the injured woman tried to protest that someone else had already promised the same thing, they'd just shush her. "No, not to mention it. You be quiet and get your rest."

The women kept coming and coming. By the end of the third day after her fall they'd worn her down, and Malka-Vana just smiled wanly. It was no use to protest; they'd figure it out amongst themselves, she thought.

But they didn't figure it out. With the setting of the sun on the eve of Pesach came sister Shura with a basket of matzo for Malka-Vana, Reb Beno, and their children. Malka-Vana thanked her profusely and gave her some tomatoes in exchange. No sooner had Shura left than Aunt Taufel arrived with another basket of matzo. Embarrassed, Malka-Vana hid Shura's matzo in the cupboard and gratefully accepted her aunt's offering. Not an hour later, Cousin Rachel arrived with yet another basket of matzo, and then it was sister Leika, then niece Vankya, then a cousin, then another niece, then somebody's mother-in-

The Matzo Mitzvah

law whom Malka-Vana didn't even remember having met before. It went on like that until well after dark the following day, and Malka-Vana's cupboards were literally stuffed with matzo.

For the next week, the entire eight days of Pesach, the family ate almost nothing but matzo. They had matzo for breakfast, matzo for lunch, matzo for dinner, matzo for snacks, and matzo at teatime. At their seder they stuffed themselves with matzo until they gagged on it and puffed up like balloons. Toward the end of the week, as Malka-Vana was bathing her youngest child, Itzik, she was horrified to find a thick white crust inside his ears. God forbid! The boy had matzo coming out his ears!

They ate all they could, for it would be a shande to let any of the sacred matzo go to waste, but of course it was hopeless. At the end of the week there seemed to be even more matzo left over than they had started with, and what had begun as a mitzvah had now become a problem: what to do with all that leftover matzo? They couldn't just throw it away. And, God help them, they couldn't eat any more.

As soon as the holiday had ended, Reb Beno took all the leftover matzo and stuffed it into a huge flour sack and, careful that none of the relatives should see him, carried it to Rabbi Shmul. Surely the rabbi would know how to dispose of this mitzvah run amok.

But my great-great-grandfather just stared at the sack and scratched his scraggly beard. Reb Beno suggested donating it to the poor, but Rabbi Shmul didn't think it was a good idea. "True," he said, "we have many poor in our ghetto. But they, too, have been eating matzo for a week already, and just like everyone else they're so sick of it they'd rather eat newspaper. Being poor doesn't affect the taste buds, you know. No, from such a mitzvah no one should suffer."

Then suddenly a light came on in Grandpa's eyes. "Beno," he said, "I have an idea. Why not take the matzo to the forest and donate it to the animals? Sure, it's a little stale by now, but you can hardly tell the difference. And the animals aren't picky eaters, anyway. Just think what a mitzvah it would be to share our matzo with God's creatures of the forest. Why, they could have their own animal seder—a few days late, perhaps, but a Pesach celebration nonetheless."

It seemed a wonderful solution, and Reb Beno slung the sack of leftover matzo over his shoulder and set out at once for the forest. Though the bag was heavy, his heart felt light to be doing such a kindness to the dumb animals, and his stomach was glad just to be rid of all that matzo.

But unbeknownst to Reb Beno, there was a small hole in the bottom of the sack full of matzo. He didn't notice the little pile of crumbs it left on the floor of the rabbi's parlor, and he didn't notice

The Matzo Mitzvah

the thin but steady trail of matzo that spread behind him as he walked. And he certainly never noticed that the huge sack was just a bit lighter when he arrived at the forest.

In a clearing in the woods he upended the sack, broke the cakes of matzo into small pieces, and spread the crumbs out on the ground. It looked like it had snowed, he thought, there was so much matzo. "There you are, animals," he said. "Enjoy."

That done, Reb Beno pulled his ear lobe three times and immediately left the forest; for like all the ghettoites he held the wilderness in superstitious awe and would not remain one moment longer than was absolutely necessary.

That seemed to be the end of the affair. Malka-Vana was up and around again, on crutches that Dr. Shatsky had loaned her, and her first order of business was to bake an ovenful of real leavened bread. But just as her family was finishing its first non-matzo meal in over a week, they were interrupted by a strange scratch-scratching sound outside the kitchen door. Reb Beno went to see what it was, and when he opened the door he was surprised to find two beautiful ring-necked pheasants pecking at a pile of matzo crumbs on the stoop. They looked up at him gratefully and said, "Klook, klook," then went back to their scratching and pecking.

For the first time Reb Beno realized what had happened: the pheasants had followed the trail of matzo from the clearing where he had dumped his offering, all the way back to his very door. He tried to shoo them back to the forest, but already they were so stuffed they couldn't fly; they couldn't even walk. Even after the matzo was all gone, they just sat there going "Klook, klook."

Now, Reb Beno had often heard that roasted pheasant was a gourmet treat relished by the nobility, who sent hunting parties into the woods and fields to shoot the birds. But since meat killed in a hunt was not kosher, neither Reb Beno nor any of the ghettoites had ever tasted this delicacy. Here, however, were two plump birds who seemed to be offering themselves to him, perhaps in thanks for the Pesach meal he had donated to their kind.

Reb Beno picked up the pheasants, who were either too grateful or too stuffed with matzo to offer the least resistance. He put them into the sack he had used to carry the matzo, and carried them to Reb Vilhik, the shochet. Reb Vilhik was surprised. He had never seen a pheasant before, much less slaughtered one. But when Reb Beno pressed him, he admitted that it couldn't be any different from preparing a chicken, and so he set to work. In less than an hour Reb Beno was on his way back home with two perfectly dressed, strictly kosher large birds, and that same evening

Malka-Vana roasted them to a golden brown.

The next morning Reb Beno went around to the homes of the relatives who had provided his family with such an abundance of matzo and gave each of them a piece of roasted pheasant. There were so many of them that no one got very much, but surely they were as responsible as anyone for the mitzvah that had shown up pecking on his doorway, and they were entitled. He saved the best piece, however, for Rabbi Shmul, whose idea it had been, and to him and Rebbitsin Helga he gave an entire golden-brown breast.

"Delicious," said my great-great-grandfather as he licked the last tasty morsel from his lips, and his wife could only agree.

"You know," he said reflectively, as was his wont when his stomach was full, "there is an old saying: If you cast your bread upon the sea, good fortune will return to you. Maybe we should adapt this saying for our own ghetto: If you cast your matzo in the forest, a mitzvah will surely come to your door!"

The Rabbi and the Soldier

My great-great-grandfather, Rabbi Shmul, and my great-great-grandmother, Rebbitsin Helga, were in their early thirties when they were blessed with twin boys. The older, by several minutes, they named Shlomo, after Shmul's father, and the younger they named Yuskala Chaim, after Helga's father. Many years later, when I was born, I was named after the younger twin, Chaim, which in English is Herman.

By the time the boys turned sixteen, they had already decided what they would like to do in life.

Shlomo wanted to become a rabbi, like his namesake and his father, and Yuskala Chaim aspired to become an astronomer. Both boys were bright and diligent, and no one doubted that they would achieve their goals.

Then one of life's unanticipated tragedies occurred. Late one afternoon Captain Magirkik of the Orsha police knocked on my great-great-grandparents' door, and as soon as Grandpa answered it, he could see that the captain brought bad news. An order had come from army headquarters in Moscow stating that Yuskala Chaim was to be drafted into the Russian army.

It might as well have been a death warrant. If there was one thing that Russia's Jews feared more than anything—more than plagues, more than sin, more than the depredations of the Cossacks—it was induction into the army. Soldiers, Jew or gentile, were drafted for twenty-five-year hitches; but few Jews ever returned. In fact, most were never heard from again. In later years, many Jews, including my own father, left their homes and families and emigrated to foreign lands precisely to avoid being drafted into the army.

Yuskala Chaim's fate seemed sealed. It would be the first time that the twins had been separated, and this only added to the grief that consumed the entire family—nay, the entire shtetl. But despite the firm friendship that Grandpa and the captain had enjoyed for many years, there was no way around it. The captain must execute his order, and Yuskala Chaim was to become a soldier. Thus it was that a grievously tearful farewell was held at the Orsha train station, and Yuskala Chaim went to do his duty.

The house seemed dead after that. Even though the draft board had somehow overlooked Shlomo, it was as if Yuskala Chaim had taken his brother's lust for life with him; for without his lifelong companion and playmate, Shlomo was transformed overnight from a boisterous boy to a melancholy man. Holidays were particularly difficult.

Then one day a letter arrived. It wasn't a happy letter, but even the news that Yuskala Chaim was alive was cause for celebration. The brief note read as follows:

> My Dear Family,
> Please know that I am alive and still in the army, and doing as well as could be hoped. I am with a unit in Comeralsky, in the western part of our country. The routine is very hard, and the Russian soldiers treat me like a dog. They give me and the few other Jews in our unit the jobs that they do not like for themselves, and we must comply for fear of a beating, or even worse. Nevertheless, I have managed to make a few

friends here among the other Jews and even a few of the Russians.

How is the family? I hope Shlomo is studying hard for the rabbinate. I cannot think anymore of my desire to study astronomy; it is too hard.

The officers in charge have told us again and again that we may not send letters home, and I am taking quite some risk in doing so anyway. I am giving this letter to a Jewish man I met in Comeralsky, who has agreed to deliver it, for the military would never do so. I hope he is not discovered, for if he were, things would go badly for him as well as for me. If I can make contact with him again, or with other people of good heart, I shall write to you again as often as I am able.

I send you my love, and please remember me to my friends back in dear old Orsha.

Your loving son,
Yuskala Chaim

Sad to relate, that was the very last word they received from Yuskala Chaim, my great-uncle. Perhaps he tried to write again and was discovered; perhaps he died in the service of Mother Russia. Several times Rabbi Shmul, with the help of Captain Magirkik, tried to glean some news of his son from the authorities; but he might as well have asked the stones. Such information, he was curtly told, was classified. His letters to Moscow went unanswered, and once when he went in person to the office of the head of the Cossacks, their captain seemed only to laugh at him. "He's just a private, and a Jew; we don't keep track of such pettiness. Anyway, you should be proud of him; a soldier's life will make a man of him."

But life goes on despite its hardships, and indeed for the best of us, hardship only strengthens the resolve to persevere. So it was with Shlomo, who put away his childish games and devoted himself body and soul to his studies. Just a few weeks after his brother had left to join the army, Rabbi Shmul and Rebbitsin Helga decided that it would be best for Shlomo to get out of the house and continue his studies under another rabbi. A change of scene might do him good. Perhaps then he could forget his loneliness and grief.

In the nearby village of Votlishkoff lived a good friend of my great-great-grandparents, Rabbi Sheizel, an old and very learned rabbi, and it was to him that they entrusted their remaining son. They arranged for Shlomo not only to study with Rabbi Sheizel, but to take room and board in the rabbi's home as well. And so it was that another tearful farewell was staged at the Orsha railway station—this one, however, filled with hope and promise.

Things went well for Shlomo from the very first. The rabbi and his wife, Rebbitsin Rosishka, had never had children of their own, and they took Shlomo into their home with glee. In no time they were like family. Shlomo told the rabbi all about his family, especially about his father, whom Rabbi Sheizel had not seen in many years, and as time passed he again became the cheerful young man he had been before his brother was drafted.

For his part, Rabbi Sheizel planned a two-year course of study for the boy. It was perhaps an unusually difficult and complex syllabus, and the rabbi was perhaps more strict with Shlomo than he would have been with another student. But it was not out of meanness, or anything like that; it was just that he wanted more than anything that the son of his old friend should not only succeed, but excel.

Toward the end of the second year, as Shlomo was nearing the end of his studies and looking forward to ordination as a full-fledged rabbi, tragedy again fell out of the sky and struck right next to him. It was a hot day in August, and Shlomo and Rabbi Sheizel were walking to the nearby village of Vincova to visit a woman who was ill. About halfway to Vincova they came upon an overturned wagon in the middle of the road.

"Help me!" cried a voice from under the wagon. Shlomo and Rabbi Sheizel ran to help, and they discovered that the voice belonged to Reb Kvalitch, who had been pinned under the wagon when the axle broke and the whole affair toppled over.

Now, Shlomo was still a skinny teenager, but Rabbi Sheizel was a bear of a man, and this would not be the first wagon he had ever lifted. So while Shlomo held the horse, Rabbi Sheizel bent down, grabbed the broken axle and heaved with all his might.

Reb Kvalitch slithered out from under the wreck and seemed to be okay; but unfortunately the rabbi was not. He dropped the wagon as soon as Reb Kvalitch got clear of it, then stood at the roadside sweating profusely. Before he could sit down, he collapsed in a heap, stricken with a heart attack. Shlomo and Reb Kvalitch were frantic. They stripped off the heavy black coat that the rabbi always wore no matter the weather, and mopped his brow. "My arm..." moaned Rabbi Sheizel. Then he passed out.

"Quick," said Shlomo, "run to the village and get help!" Reb Kvalitch left immediately, and he was back with three other men in just a few minutes. But they were too late, and there was nothing to be done. Rabbi Sheizel was dead.

The news came hard to the residents of Votlishkoff. Rabbi Sheizel had been their rabbi for more than thirty years, the only rabbi many of the people had ever known. Black crepe appeared in every window, torn lapels dangled from every coat, and the Shiva service was attended by everyone in the ghetto and more than a few Russians from the town. Afterwards it seemed the entire world sat shiva as one.

When the mourning period had ended, the elders of Votlishkoff met to consider the problem of finding a new rabbi. There was much discussion, and their leader, Reb Solomon, was the first to offer a solution.

"What about Shlomo? He was Rabbi Sheizel's favorite student. He's practically finished his studies and is ready to become a rabbi. As you all know, Rabbi Sheizel, olev hasholem, always spoke very highly of him and considered him almost his own son. Let us ask Shlomo to remain here in Votlishkoff and become our rabbi."

Impossible as it sounds, for once everyone agreed instantly.

Reb Solomon and a couple of the others made the proposition to Shlomo. At first Shlomo was unsure. How could he hope to fill the shoes of his wise teacher? Furthermore, he had always hoped to return to his hometown, Orsha, and relieve his own father of his duties there.

But the elders implored him, and finally Shlomo agreed. He wrote to his parents in Orsha telling them what had happened and asking their blessing to become the rabbi of Votlishkoff. Although Rabbi Shmul and Rebbitsin Helga were heartbroken to hear of the death of their old friend, they were bursting with pride for their son, and encouraged him to accept.

Thus it was that my great-grandfather, Rabbi Shlomo, followed in the footsteps of his father and his father's father and became the rabbi and leader of the shtetl of Votlishkoff, a position he held until his death some fifty years later. To describe those fifty years would require another book even longer than this one; but there is just one incident that must be related here.

Shlomo never forgot his brother, of course, who had aspired to become an astronomer. Although Shlomo had never had any particular affinity for the physical sciences, he made the study of stars and planets a lifelong hobby, in remembrance of his brother. One spring evening during the celebration of Succoth, he was lying on his back in a field near his home in Votlishkoff, admiring the constellations and thinking of his brother, Yuskala Chaim. Maybe he was up there now, he mused, among the stars, in heaven.

Then he noticed a group of stars he had not noticed before. At first he thought it was Orion, but when he looked more carefully he saw that it was not. Whereas Orion is posed arching his bow and aiming his arrow toward the east, this star-man looked like he was shouldering a rifle, and facing west.

A soldier, Shlomo thought, just like my brother, my poor lost brother, who was sent to the west and never came back. A soldier marching through heaven.

And so he named the constellation for his soldier twin whom he would never see again; he named it Yuskala Chaim. And although it doesn't appear on any star chart, that's how it has been known among the Jews of Byelorussia ever since.

The star-soldier winked at my great-grandfather and marched off across the sky, going west, toward America.